PRAISE FOR *MOMMY'S ANGEL*

"Miasha keeps things moving at a fast clip, but the basic empathy and understanding that pervade are the story's real appeal. [She] never loses sight of the basic humanity of all the lost souls that surround Angel."

—*Publishers Weekly*

"In the midst of all the same voices in literature, Miasha brings authenticity to the pages of this novel. She's the crème de la crème—enjoy!"

—Vickie Stringer, *Essence* bestselling author of
Let That Be the Reason

"*Mommy's Angel* highlights some of the harsh realities that many of our society's poor and forgotten children face in life. . . . Earthy, realistic, and full of unpredictable twists and turns, Miasha has written a novel that is sure to please."

—Rawsistaz.com

"*Mommy's Angel* is a fast-paced, well-written, realistic view of what addiction does to our communities. It sheds a bright light on how the addict's hurt, pain, and trouble are recycled onto the people closest to them."

—Danielle Santiago, author of *Grindin'* and
Essence #1 bestseller *Little Ghetto Girl*

"A poignant tale of innocence lost in Brooklyn."
—K'wan, author of *Gangsta, Street Dreams, Eve,* and *Hood Rat*

PRAISE FOR *DIARY OF A MISTRESS*

"Miasha cleverly builds up the suspense and throws in several unexpected twists. Her latest release is filled with intrigue and will keep you turning the pages. *Diary of a Mistress* will make you think twice about who you trust."
—Sheila M. Goss, e-Spire Entertainment News editor and author of *My Invisible Husband*

"Miasha has done it again. *Diary of a Mistress* is a sizzling novel full of unexpected twists and guaranteed to leave readers in shock, and gasping for air, as they excitedly turn each page."
—Karen E. Quinones Miller, author of *Satin Doll, I'm Telling,* and *Satin Nights*

"*Diary of a Mistress* is an intense, captivating, and twisted love triangle. Miasha allows the usually silent mistress to raise her voice through the pages of her diary."
—Daaimah S. Poole, author of *Ex-Girl to the Next Girl, What's Real,* and *Got a Man*

"Only Miasha can make it hard to choose between wanting to be the mistress or the wife."
—Brenda L. Thomas, author of *Threesome, Fourplay,* and *The Velvet Rope*

PRAISE FOR *SECRET SOCIETY*

"Scandalous and engrossing, this debut from Miasha . . . shows her to be a writer to watch."
—*Publishers Weekly*

ALSO BY MIASHA

Never Enough
Sistah for Sale
Mommy's Angel
Diary of a Mistress
Secret Society

CHASER

MIASHA

A Touchstone Book
Published by Simon & Schuster
New York   London   Toronto   Sydney

TOUCHSTONE
A Division of Simon & Schuster, Inc.
1230 Avenue of the Americas
New York, NY 10020

This book is a work of fiction. Names, characters, places, and incidents either are products of the author's imagination or are used fictitiously. Any resemblance to actual events or locales or persons, living or dead, is entirely coincidental.

Designed by Jamie Kerner

Manufactured in the United States of America

ISBN 978-1-61523-144-7

To the newest addition to my family, Ace Nasir.
Getting this done has been a long journey,
and I'm blessed to have had you to be a part of it
Love you, baby boy,
Mommy

Leah

KENNY, STOP, PLEEEEASE! KENNNNYYY!" I cried for my
life. It wasn't even about the baby anymore because I was sure it
was dead. There was no way it could have withstood the blows
Kenny delivered directly to my stomach. Not to mention his dragging
me around on the concrete floors. My poor baby was gone. I was feeling weaker with each punch. I was losing consciousness, and I realized
Kenny was trying to kill me.

"Please, Kenny, don't kill me," I said with what little energy I had.
"Please."

Kenny turned me over on my back and straddled my neck and
upper chest. He looked in my eyes as I gagged for air. He was blurry
to me. In fact, everything was blurry. I turned to my right and the
door to one of the guest bedrooms was opened. The furniture in it

looked like it was floating. All of the colors from the sage-colored paint on the walls to the olive-green silk drapes on the windows and the multicolored Oriental rugs on the hardwood floors blended together, forming one big rainbow cloud. When I looked up at the recessed lights that lined the ceiling in our hallway, I felt nauseous. I wanted to close my eyes to avoid the dizzy feeling I had, but I was afraid if I did I would die. So I fought with all my might to keep my eyelids from drooping. And just as I was beginning to give up on trying to stay alive, I felt Kenny's weight lift off me and heard him walking away from me and down the stairs. I felt a sense of relief, as I believed he was finished with me.

I had a moment to think about everything I had done to end up in the position I was in, and I wondered if it was worth it. Was it really worth my life? I wished I could turn back the hands of time, but I couldn't, and before I wasted any more time pitying myself, I needed to focus on what I could do to get help.

Relief was short-lived. As I lay there on the cold hardwood floor, clinging to consciousness, I could faintly hear Kenny's footsteps once again on the steps.

I opened my eyes as much as my strength would allow and saw Kenny pouring what I figured was gasoline on every step as he walked backward down our spiral staircase. I wanted to protest, to try to plead for my life, but I had no energy at all to do or say anything. I felt completely paralyzed, helpless, as good as dead.

"This'll teach you to wear a wire on me, bitch!" Kenny yelled.

Then I heard the sound of the gasoline can being dropped at the bottom of the steps and, seconds later, a loud poof. A panic came over me. My mind was telling me to get up and run, but my body wouldn't move. I thought about my mom and how she'd tried to tell me time and time again to leave Kenny alone. Had I listened to her, I would not have been preparing to meet my death. I thought about Nasir and wondered what he would say and how he would feel once he found out that I was gone. I wished I could have had one last moment with him. Even if it was just to say good-bye. My life nearing its end, I began to muffle the Twenty-third Psalm.

"The Lord is my shepherd; I shall not want. He maketh me to lie down in green pastures: he leadeth me beside the still waters. He restoreth my soul: he leadeth me in the paths of righteousness for his name's sake. Yea, though I walk through the valley of death, I will fear no evil: for thou art with me; thy rod and thy staff they comfort me. Thou preparest a table before me in the presence of mine enemies: thou anointest my head with oil; my cup runneth over. Surely goodness and mercy shall follow me all the days of my life, and I will dwell in the house of the Lord for ever."

I closed my eyes. I thought about the date: May 30, 2008. So my tombstone would read Leah Cecily Nicole Baker, July 17, 1983, to May 30, 2008. Then I had second thoughts. I'm not ready to die and especially not like this. I want to fight. I want to fight badly. But I can't. Please, God, spare my life. Please, God, intervene. Please don't let today be my last.

Leah

Five Months Earlier

was in bed asleep when Kenny came home with another one of his schemes. Over the last year that we'd been living together, this had gotten to be a pattern. But usually he was a lot nicer and sweeter than he was tonight. He used to cuddle up with me and tell me what he was planning and what role he needed me to play. He always had a hustle up his sleeve, too, and it seemed his hustles got grander with time. He went from using stolen gas cards and fillin' niggas' tanks up for half price to sellin' phony master's degrees to rich white kids who'd rather spend their tuition on crystal meth and prescription drugs. And who do you think sold them the crystal meth and pills? Kenny, of course. He was a one-stop shop. But I couldn't knock him. His desire to make money afforded me a pretty good lifestyle. And if I didn't love him for anything else, I loved Kenny for taking care of me.

"Get up, Leah. Get dressed real quick," he demanded as he turned on the bedroom light and pulled the covers off me.

I lifted the eye mask off my eyes and asked, "Why, what's the problem?"

"I got something I need you to do. Hurry up, 'cause everybody outside waiting."

I sat up in our California king bed and scooted over to my side. I reached to pick up my cell phone off the charging station that sat on the European-style nightstand. I looked at the screen. "It's one o'clock in the morning," I whined.

"I know what time it is. Hurry up and throw some clothes on," he said with energy, as if it were one in the afternoon.

He grabbed me by my arm and assisted me out the bed. I closed my eyes again, hoping he would get the hint and leave me alone. He didn't. Instead, he walked me into our master bathroom. I could tell because of the warmth I felt under my feet from the bathroom's heated marble floors. He ran some water in the sink, splashing some on my face. Finally, I opened my eyes. Immediately upon doing so, I grabbed the remote out of its base off the wall and dimmed the recessed lights. My eyes weren't ready for bright lights just yet.

"You're wetting my hair!" I complained. "You know I don't get perms no more!"

"My bad. I just need you to move like you got somewhere to be. Time is money."

"What do you have me doin', Kenny?" I asked, drying my face with one of the hand towels I kept rolled up in a basket on top of the marble counter.

"I'll explain it to you in the car. Get dressed and meet me in the garage," Kenny said before he left the bedroom.

I threw on a Juicy sweatsuit and some UGG boots. I unwrapped my hair and ran my fingers through it to allow the loose curls to fall into place. I didn't have time to put on makeup, so lip gloss and eyeliner it was. I grabbed the gold Gucci handbag I had carried earlier in the day because it already had my wallet and keys inside. Otherwise, I would have taken one of my Louis bags, which would have coordinated better with what I was wearing.

I dragged my feet down our long hallway, smirking at the black-and-white pictures of just about every gangster known to man—outlaws both fictional and non—that lined the walls. Every time I passed the artwork, I found it amusing that characters like Vito Corleone and Scarface were Kenny's role models. I walked past the front staircase and proceeded to the back one, which led straight to our kitchen. When I got downstairs, I stopped at our Viking stainless steel refrigerator and grabbed a Red Bull. I needed a boost of energy. There was no telling what Kenny was going to have me do. I walked into the three-car garage, and Kenny was in the passenger side of our 2007 Range Rover Sport. The engine was already running. I heard the doors unlock and took that as my cue to get in. I opened the driver's-side door, which required extra tugging since it had been side swiped a few months before. We had had every intention on getting it fixed, but Kenny wound up spending the check from the insurance company. He claimed he was going to put the money back in an account, but he never did. He blew the money, which was something he did frequently. That was why every so often he would rely on a scam to build his stash up again. He was good at making money but not so good at keeping it, and therefore he spent more time chasing it than enjoying it.

Kenny and I had been together for a little over three years—longer than I ever expected. When I first met him, I figured he would be somebody I would just have fun with. You know, go to the movies, have dinner, just kick it with him from time to time. But it so happened that eight months into our relationship my older sister's drinking became a nuisance. We would fight constantly over her stealing my money and personal belongings. I wanted to move out of my mom's house so that I wouldn't have to keep going through drama with my sister, but I didn't have enough money to be on my own. Moving in with Kenny was my solution. And what started off as a friendship-with-benefits type of situation turned into a courtship.

"Why are we driving this? The door hardly opens, and it's all crashed up on the side."

" 'Cause we're gettin' rid of it tonight," he said. "Now, drive to Fifth and Spring Garden."

I put the SUV in drive and pulled out of the garage. Once on the street, I noticed a car following us. As I turned left on Saint Asaphs and sped up, the other car did, too. I took the winding road around until it dead-ended at City Avenue. I got in the left-turn-only lane, and sure enough the car behind me did the same.

"Who's that behind me?" I asked, looking in my rearview mirror.

Without budging to see who it was, Kenny responded, "It's my cousin Dahwoo and his girl. Once we get to where we're goin', they're goin' to get in the backseat."

"Okay, so what's goin' on? Why did you get me out of bed?"

"Listen, we goin' drive to a low-key area where it's not a lot of traffic. Once we get there, we goin' get out the car and stand to the side while my man drive the car into a wall—"

"What?" I cut him off.

"Just listen. Then you goin' get back in the driver's seat, I'm goin' get back in the passenger seat, and Dahwoo and his girl goin' get in the back. You're goin' call the cops and tell them you were just in an accident."

"Are you serious?" I asked him, unable to hold my peace any longer. "And what's the point in doing this?"

"For one, I'm tired of payin' a note and insurance on a car we don't drive. For two, I'm goin' get a cut off the check the insurance company goin' write to fix it. And for three, me, you, Woo, and his girl goin' rack up on case money."

"Oh my God."

"Now, listen," he continued. "You goin' tell the police that you were driving and a car turned left out of nowhere, hitting you on your driver's side, forcing you to turn the wheel suddenly. You wounded up losing control and you ran into the wall."

"I don't understand, Kenny. What are you having me do?"

"It's simple, Leah. Just do what I say and trust me, all right? We don't have a lot of time. Soon the streets goin' be flooded with niggas leavin' the clubs. Now Nasir is goin' be there to tow the car. Act like you don't know him other than the fact that he's a tow-truck driver and you want him to tow your car."

"How is it that you always manage to drag Nasir in the middle of your schemes?"

"Damn, do it fuckin' matter?" Kenny snapped. "You startin' to get on my nerves with all the questions and doubts and shit."

I sighed and said, "Okay. Whatever." And left it at that. *Poor Nasir*, I thought. He was so sweet and reserved. And Kenny seemed to take advantage of him, always getting him to do favors for him. I never understood why Nasir wouldn't just tell Kenny no sometimes. It was obvious that he wanted to. But he seemed to be as controlled by Kenny as I was these days. It wasn't always like that, though. When I met Kenny, he and Nasir were real cool. They both chased car wrecks for Nasir's dad, Vic, who owned one of the biggest and most popular auto-body shops in Philly—Alliance Collision, up on Cedar Avenue. They made good money, too, no less than two thousand a week, and that was when it had been a slow week. But about two years ago Kenny decided he wanted more, so he started dabbling in the drug game. His older brother Tim was a known dealer, and when he got locked up, he needed somebody to take over for him and hold him down until he got out. Kenny seized the opportunity. And instead of just holding his brother down, he made moves to bring his brother up. He realized that the more variety you had, the more money you could make. So he didn't limit himself to weed and cocaine like his competitors did. He sold everything from crystal meth, ketamine or Special K, roofies, and acid to pills like codeine, Roxys, and Oxy-Contin. After a short while he no longer needed the money he got from chasing, but he didn't quit because chasing was his front. Plus, he benefited from being able to store his drugs in Vic's shop. It seemed like he had become a kingpin overnight. And with that title came loads of money, notoriety, and haters.

Kenny's newfound fame and fortune made him a target not only for the police but for the stick-up kids who robbed drug dealers for a living. Eventually Kenny drew a whole lot of attention to Vic's shop. He made it hot. Cops would ride by frequently. Vic was suspicious and would ask Kenny if he was hustling, but Kenny would deny it. But one day the shop got robbed at gunpoint by some guys in masks, and all of Kenny's drugs were taken, proving Vic's suspicions. After that Vic fired Kenny. He was pissed off that Kenny had jeopardized his employees' lives and his business, and Vic told him that if he ever put anything of Vic's in harm's way again, he would kill his ass.

Kenny been doin' the drug thing full-time ever since. And he had gotten so good at it that when his brother Tim came home from doing a seven-month bid, Kenny wound up being his boss.

Nasir, on the other hand, kept with the chasing and seemed to try to stay out of trouble. But Kenny tends to keep him in some shit, always dragging him in on his illegal activities.

I got to Fifth and Spring Garden at a quarter to two. It was deserted, not common since it was up the street from Fuzion nightclub and down the street from Transit and Palmers. There weren't even a lot of people in Silk City diner, which sat right on the corner. Being a weeknight in January had everything to do with there being so few people out, I was sure.

I pulled over while Kenny's cousin Dahwoo parked his older-model Pontiac Grand Prix on a side street off Fifth. He and his girl-friend, whom I had never met before, got in with Kenny and me. We took Fifth Street a couple blocks up, passing Green and then Wallace Street until we were at Fairmount Avenue.

"Pull over right here," Kenny said.

What the hell? Of all hoods to do what we were about to do, why did Kenny pick this one? I was uneasy about executing Kenny's plan as it was. But on top of that, we were doing it smack dead in the hood. My nerves were shot.

I quickly pressed the lock button when I noticed a tall, slinky guy who had a bounce in his step walking over toward our car. He was dressed in dark colors and looked like he was a smoker—untrustworthy.

"He's cool," Kenny said as the guy approached my side. Kenny leaned over my seat to give him a handshake through the rolled-down window. Then Kenny instructed us all to get out of the car. The guy then got in the driver's seat. Meanwhile, the four of us stood on the sidewalk while the guy deliberately drove my Range Rover head-on into an abandoned building's wall. Seeing that it wasn't hit hard enough, Kenny instructed the guy to do it once more, this time with more gas.

The guy did what he was told, completing his part of the plan. After the car was successfully planted into the wall, he jumped out and approached Kenny, who placed some money in his palm. The guy then took off through an alley. At that, we were on. We all followed Kenny's lead as he got back into the car.

Unlike Dahwoo's girl, who was giggling and telling jokes in the backseat about what had just gone down, I didn't find anything funny. I actually had a bad feeling about everything. Then it dawned on me that Kenny, Dahwoo, and I were committing a federal crime with this chick, whom I was sure none of us knew well enough to trust. I mean, that was my first time meeting her, and just last week Dahwoo was calling a different girl his wife. For all we knew, this bitch could have been an undercover. She could have been setting us up. Or even if she wasn't, if we got caught, who was to say that she wouldn't rat us all out to save her own ass.

My negative thoughts got the best of me, and suddenly I panicked and froze up, forgetting everything I was supposed to do.

"Call the police," Kenny yelled, taking me out of paralysis.

I pulled my cell phone from my pocketbook and dialed 911. It was a good thing I was in a panic because it made my reporting of the accident sound so damn real. The dispatcher said she would send out an officer.

Chasers arrived on the scene in packs—some in tow trucks, others in cars. That was the game for you. I could just imagine their being posted at a location nearby, listening to the police scanners waiting for an accident to be called. And when they heard Fifth and Fairmount, they all hauled ass over here, hoping they would be the first to the scene and be able to convince me to let them take my car to a body shop they were contracted with. And they were deep, too—about eight of them, all representing a different type of chaser. One was big and grimy looking, dressed in a Dickies and Timbs, getting out of a dirty eagle claw with chipped lettering on the side. Another one was clean-cut, dressed in a black mink coat with a pair of black Nike boots, Rock and Republic jeans, and black Gucci scully. And he had the nerve to jump out of a Mercedes-Benz CLS. Niggas killed me, chasin' out of luxury cars. But I must admit, if I was really in an accident and I didn't already have chaser in mind to take my car, I would have chosen to go with dude in the Benz. I would've felt more comfortable handing my car over to somebody who didn't look like he needed money rather than to somebody grimy-looking. Maybe it was just me, but I felt like somebody who didn't need money would be less likely to rip me off.

Among the chasers was Nasir, who was the one I agreed to let tow my car, of course. The other chasers were angry that Nasir was on their territory. See, Nasir chased out West Philly and Southwest, in the vicinity of his dad's shop. So for him to be up North Philly runnin' a hit was frowned upon. And generally chasers respected the boundaries—not necessarily because it was the right thing to do, but because it wasn't logical for a chaser to run a hit that was far from where he posted up. For one, he could program his police scanner to receive calls only in the specific district in which he chased. And for two, a chaser never knew what would be at a hit and whether it was worth his showing up. For example, it could be a minor fender bender, a totaled vehicle, or an unfounded, which meant there was nothing there at all. So it wasn't worth it for a chaser to drive to an uncertain situation far away and risk missing a real hit close by.

But in this case, it was different. Nasir was in on our plan. And because I made it clear that I wanted nobody but Nasir to touch my car, the other chasers had no choice but to fall back.

The police pulled up, and there were two squad cars instead of one. Four officers got out—three males and one female. They walked over to us as we remained seated in the Range. I was preparing my story in my head, and I was starting to feel a little better about things— safer now that the police were there and even credible, since all the tow trucks out there were creating a realistic-looking accident scene.

"Hi, ma'am," one officer said to me.

"Hello."

"Are you all all right?" he asked, looking at each person in the car.

"Yes," we said.

"My neck is stiff," Dahwoo's girl said from behind me; she sounded rehearsed.

"What happened?" the officer then asked, not seeming the least bit concerned about any injuries.

I described what was supposed to have happened. I was only sentences into the story Kenny had told me to deliver to the cops when a second officer stopped me.

"That's all we need to hear," she said, rolling her eyes. "Have them step out of the vehicle."

I was a bit confused at that point, because I expected the cops to be more sensitive toward accident victims. Instead, she seemed aggravated.

"I'm gonna need you four to step out of the vehicle," one male officer said.

Each of us reluctantly exited the Range. Right away the four officers grabbed hold of the four of us and placed us under arrest. My heart sank. I looked at Dahwoo's girl to see her reaction. If she was too calm, then my earlier feelings about her setting us up were most likely correct. But she looked just as shocked, confused, and scared as I felt. I looked at Dahwoo, then at Kenny. They, too, were confused. Immediately, we all started asking questions: What did we do? What were we getting locked up for? Could we call our attorneys? Anything we could think of to ask to stall being hauled off to jail. And when the questions were not getting us anywhere with the cops, we started accusing the police of profiling us.

The female cop who seemed aggravated by all the questions said, "You would pick the corner that's being surveilled to pull off your fake little accident, wouldn't you?"

With that, our questions were answered. Apparently, the corner we were on was being watched for drug activity by a stakeout team, and they'd gotten more than they'd bargained for that night as they witnessed our scheme from beginning to end. We were all handcuffed and taken to the Sixth Police District.

"Who put you up to this?" the interrogating officer asked me again, after supposedly going back and speaking with Kenny, Dahwoo, and Dahwoo's girl.

His appearance was intimidating—big, bulky body; deep-set blue eyes; anger-red flesh tone—but the way he talked to me wasn't. He was calm and endearing, like he wanted to reason with me. But I didn't buy his niceness. I figured it was just a technique to get me to feel comfortable opening up to him.

"I said, 'nobody.' "

"So you planned this on your own? Because I have to tell you, that's what everybody's saying. They're saying *you* put them up to this. But I have a hard time believing that, because you just don't strike me as the type that would put yourself in this predicament. But you know, if you don't wanna talk, I can always go off what the others have told me."

"I'd rather talk to an attorney," I said, standing my ground.

"Okay, fine," he said. "Here's my card, in case you decide you want to start standing up for yourself."

I smirked at his final attempt to get me to talk but said nothing further.

He slid his business card across the table and left the room. I put my head down on the table and tried to register what Kenny had got me into this time. Fucking with Kenny, there was never a dull moment. In fact, I spent two of the three years that we've been together going through bullshit on his account. From shoot-outs to drama from the bitches he would mess with behind my back, it was always something.

I wondered when I would get tired of it all and leave him. But every time the thought to leave came across my mind, I felt burdened. I mean, before Kenny I was self-sufficient. I was going to school and I had two jobs. But once I got with Kenny, I slowly started to get used to not working and not going to school. And it wasn't like I just got lazy all of a sudden. But Kenny would entice me to miss days at work and school. For example, he would offer to pay me triple for the hours I missed at work if I spent that time with him instead. Overall, Kenny took good care of me. I grew accustomed to a luxury lifestyle, and before long I found myself solely dependent on him. So it wasn't easy for me to pick up and leave him when I felt like I wanted to. I always found myself asking the same questions: What would I do without

Kenny? Where would I live? What would I drive? How would I support myself? Ultimately, I felt like I was stuck with him.

I was placed in a cell alone. I was surprised, too, because I thought they would put Dahwoo's girl and me together, since we were both females. I wanted to ask her some questions, get inside her head a little bit to make sure she could be trusted. I guessed that was the exact reason why they hadn't put us together.

Six hours passed before I was granted a phone call. I used it to call my mom.

"Hello," my mom answered in a scratchy voice.

"Ma, I'm sorry to wake you."

"Which one of my daughters is this?"

"It's Leah, Ma."

"I should've known. It better be important, Leah, calling me so early in the morning, knowing I work the graveyard shift."

I huffed and said, "Ma, I'm in jail."

"Oh Jesus, Leah. For what?"

"It's a long story, and I'd rather tell it to you in person. But what I need you to do right now is get in touch with Kenny's mom. I'm sure she knows what to do to get me out," I said.

"Why didn't you just call Kenny?"

"Well that's the thing, Ma. Kenny's in jail, too."

My mom raised her voice. "Kenny ain't in no jail. I just seen Kenny."

"You sure, Ma? I'm tellin' you, we got locked up together."

"And I'm tellin' you I just seen 'im. He was out here makin' his rounds when I got off the bus. You know he got half these kids around here sellin' for him now." My mom sounded disgusted.

A few months back Kenny dropped me off at my mom's house, and the young boys nearby were staring at Kenny's car, obviously impressed. Apparently, one of them asked Kenny what he did to make the kind of money to afford a Maserati. Kenny told him he could show him better than he could tell him and wound up turnin' the young boy and his friends on to hustling. My mom wasn't thrilled about it. She thought it was flat-out wrong that Kenny would have kids selling drugs. And on top of that, he had them selling in her apartment complex. She felt like that was a sign of disrespect toward her. The two of them had a falling-out over it and haven't spoken to each other since.

"What time was this?"

"What time is it now, like nine o'clock? So it was like a quarter to eight when I got in here."

"That's strange. He didn't say anything to you?"

"Do he ever say anything to me?"

"Well, can you call him on the three-way then?"

"Ugh," my mom made a sigh of disgust.

"This is my only call. Otherwise, I would hang up and call him myself."

"What's the number, Leah?"

I gave my mom Kenny's cell phone number. She put me on hold for a few seconds, then came back on the line.

"Hello," I heard Kenny's voice.

"Kenny!"

"Leah?"

"Yes, it's me—Leah! What you doin' out?"

"Never mind all that. How much is ya bail?" he asked.

"I don't know. I haven't seen a judge yet, which brings me back to my question. When did you see a judge? How much was ya bail?"

"I didn't go through all that, Leah. Listen, call me when you get bail. I'll be up there to get you, and we'll talk then," Kenny said in a rush.

"So it's true then, huh? Y'all put this shit on me?"

"You the only one of us that don't have a record. I'm goin' need you to take this one for the team."

"What?!" I was flabbergasted. "What do you mean take one for the team? What team? I don't have any obligations to nobody but you! I never signed up to be on a goddamn team! Why can't everybody take their own charge?" I snapped.

"Because, Leah, you'll probably get off with a couple months if you even get any time at all. If I go up, I'm looking at at least five years. The same with Woo and his girl."

"You're really serious? I don't believe you! How am I supposed to survive in jail, Kenny?"

"How would you survive out here if *I* was in jail?" He paused for a minute, I guess to let what he said penetrate. Then he proceeded, "I already put a call in to my lawyer. He'll take good care of you. He's talkin' beatin' the case."

"This is some real bullshit," I mumbled.

"Leah, it's the best situation for us right now!" Kenny protested. "If it was any other time, I wouldn't put this on you, you know that. I just can't afford a case right now. I got a deal comin' up that could retire us, baby. That could get us out the game for good and get us that vacation home out Mexico like you been wantin'. If I get locked up for this dumb shit, all that is out the window. Otherwise, I would take the charge with no problem."

I took a deep breath, still not convinced. If Kenny was so close to retiring, why would he have planned this stupid scam in the first place? Why would he have jeopardized the deal of a lifetime he supposedly had comin' up?

"Listen, let me call you back," Kenny cut off my thoughts.

"Kenny, you can't call me back! I'm in fuckin' jail!"

"Kenny, who that?" a familiar female's voice sounded.

"Was that Woo's girl?" I asked.

"Um, yeah," he said.

"What are you doin' with her?"

"I'm droppin' her off, but listen—"

" 'Droppin' her off'? That's why you rushin' me off the fuckin' phone? So you can continue to spend time with a bitch! You know what, Kenny, you ain't shit!"

"Leah, chill. Now is not the time for you to be trippin'. I know you probably emotional with all the shit that's goin' on, but I'm tellin' you, it ain't like what you takin' it as. Just call me when you get bail so I can get you outta there and we can figure everything out," Kenny said.

I huffed and said, "Okay, whatever."

Then we hung up.

"I don't believe that nigga!" I exclaimed.

"Well, you sure enough should," my mom chimed in. How much more shit you plan on takin' from that man? I mean, really. He been dumpin' his mess on you damn near y'all whole relationship. And every time somethin' go wrong, you call me. Well, I don't know what to tell you anymore. When he cheated on you, I told you to leave him. When he put his hands on you, I told you to stab his ass. Now he got you locked up while he out runnin' the streets with some chick, and I don't know *what* to tell you. I mean, granted, I don't have no big fancy house and I can't drape you in a bunch of labels and I can't put you behind the wheel of no luxury car, but I am ya mother! You can come home! You don't have to put up with his shit no more!"

"I know, Ma. I know this. But it's not that easy. When you love somebody, it's hard to just pick up and go." I had to make it seem like it was love. I couldn't just come out and tell her that the main reason I stayed with Kenny and endured his abuse was because I was financially dependent on him. That was the one thing my mom had warned me of, and I wasn't in the mood to hear I told you so.

"That's only when that somebody you love ain't yourself, Leah. Trust me, I know."

"Time's up," the officer called out.

"Ma, I gotta go. But I'm goin' call you soon as I can, okay?"

"All right, Leah. I love you."

"I love you, too, Ma."

I hung up the phone, feeling very emotional. Kenny had fucked me over, and it had my stomach in knots. How could he put this shit on me?

"Excuse me," I said to the officer who was escorting me back to my cell.

"What is it?" she asked.

"Is it possible I can speak to Detective Daily? He told me if I had any information for him to let him know."

"I'll page him."

"Thank you."

I waited anxiously to talk to the detective who had interrogated me. Finally, the time had come. I was taken out of the cell and escorted to the interrogation room. Detective Daily came in moments after I had gotten situated.

"Hello there," he said, taking a seat diagonally across from me.

I didn't speak. I just sat there in the chair goin' over my options in my head. I wanted to make sure I was doing the right thing before I opened my mouth.

"You wanted to talk?"

"Well, actually I had some questions."

"Okay."

"When you said everybody cooperated, what did you mean?"

"Cooperating means you give us all the information we ask for when we ask for it. It's simple."

I took a deep breath and massaged my temples with my fingers.

"Now, are you ready to cooperate?"

"I don't know. I know this system, and I can give y'all all the information y'all want and still wind up doing time. I need to know how I can avoid any jail time whatsoever. 'Cause everybody is lookin' out for themselves right now, and so I have to look out for me. I have to do what's best for me, and I'm tryin' to figure out what that is."

The detective leaned forward. His elbows rested on his knees as he folded his hands under his chin. "Well, you know what, Ms. Baker? Today just may be your lucky day."

I looked up at the detective. We were eye to eye. The kindness he had displayed earlier suddenly became believable. His blue eyes were filled with compassion. It was as if he knew that I was a puppet for Kenny, he knew that Kenny had been pulling my strings all along. He seemed to be able to see right through the tough facade I had put on. He knew I was vulnerable.

"How so?" I asked.

"Well, I may be able to get you a deal that involves no jail time at all."

"And what would you need from me?"

"It has nothing to do with this fraud case."

I was perplexed, and it showed on my face.

The detective continued. "Kenneth Courtland is heavily involved in the drug trade, as I'm sure you're aware. And he's someone we've been watching for some time now. We really want to nail him, but not on an insurance fraud case." The detective shook his head. "No, we want him on drug charges and the homicides that are linked to Mr. Courtland's ruthless practices."

A tear escaped my eye as I listened to the detective tell me essentially that I was in love with a monster. I mean, I knew Kenny was into what he was into, but I'd turned a blind eye to its depth. As far as I was concerned, what he did in the streets didn't affect me. Besides, it wasn't as if I'd fallen in love with Kenny the drug dealer. Like I said, when I met Kenny, he was nothing more than a wreck chaser—a young guy who was fortunate enough to make a decent living working for his best friend's dad. So I didn't feel guilty for falling in love with him. But what I had become guilty of was staying with him once he turned bad. And as the drug game changed him, he changed me. Now here I was, sucked up in his vacuum of heartache, possibly headed to federal prison for some shit he did. I felt low.

"Ms. Baker, help us help you," Detective Daily said, patting my hand.

"I don't know if I can," I cried.

"But do you really have a choice, Ms. Baker? Ask yourself that. What's goin' to happen to you if you don't help us? You're gonna go to jail, come home, and Mr. Courtland will be with someone else. I mean, the mere fact that he had another girl in the car with you is evidence of that, isn't it?"

I nodded as I recalled parts of the three-way call I'd had with my mom and Kenny: *Kenny, who that? . . . Was that Woo's girl? . . . What are you doin' with her? . . . Now he got you locked up while he out runnin' the streets with some chick . . .*

"So what are you going to do, Ms. Baker?" The detective snapped me out of my thoughts.

"I guess you're right, Detective," I mumbled. "I don't have a choice."

With those words I agreed to do something I'd never thought I would do. I agreed to be a confidential informant.

The detective coached me on what I was to do, say, and look for once I was released and back with Kenny. He also helped me concoct a story to tell Kenny about why I was getting out of jail without having to post bail.

"Kenny."

"What's up? How much is it?" he asked.

"It's steep."

"How steep?"

"Ten percent of two hundred fifty thousand."

"Damn, this your first offense! How they goin' put your bail so high? That's bullshit!"

" 'Cause they'd rather me take the deal they're offering."

"What kind of deal?" The tone in Kenny's voice grew somewhat concerned.

"You by yourself?" I asked.

"Yeah."

"Well, they said they been watching Nasir's dad for a minute. They said they know of a lot more acts of fraud that go on within his business and wreck chasing altogether. They want me to be an informant against Vic."

"Yeah?" he asked.

"That's what they said. And if I do, they said this case will disappear." I waited for Kenny's response. "Without bail," I added.

"Oh yeah?"

"Yes. So . . . I need to know what I should do."

"An informant, huh?" There was silence. "I don't know if I want my girl being so close to the law. But you know what, fuck it. I think you should take that route. Give 'em what they want. Shit, save me some money. Plus, I don't like Vic anyway. He got his shit with him."

"What about Nasir? I mean, he is your friend. You don't feel bad settin' up his father?"

"Nasir is his own man, and Vic is his own man. What Vic and I go through don't have nothin' to do with me and Nasir. Don't even worry about that."

"What if somebody finds out I'm talkin' to the cops? You know what they do to snitches in the streets."

"If it's ya time to go, you goin' go regardless. I wouldn't even worry 'bout that," he said.

Hearing his heartlessness made me sick to my stomach. He was ready and willing to throw anybody, including me, under the bus if it benefited him. That was the final straw. Kenny had showed me his true colors once and for all, and I was determined to show him mine. I loved the man, yes, but at that point I hated him equally. Besides, it was about time I started loving myself more.

Nasir

I pulled up to my dad's shop, and Brock was standing by the door shivering so bad he could barely get his cigarette to his mouth.

"It's cold than a mafucka out this mafucka," Brock said as I got out of my truck.

"I know. How long you been standin' out here?" I asked.

"Since eight o'clock, nigga—the time you was supposed to have ya ass here."

"He ain't bullshittin', either, 'cause I was out here with him," another voice called out.

I followed the voice to Kenny, who was getting out of his Maserati Quattroporte. "I woulda let him sit in my car, but that nigga wasn't willin' to put out that cigarette," Kenny said, giving me a handshake.

"Hell naw," Brock agreed. "This nigga be late every morning, havin' me stressin'. What was it this morning? You couldn't find ya hair gel?" Brock asked, taking one last puff on his cigarette, then throwing it out into the street.

"Fuck you, nigga. I got that good shit," I said, rubbing my palm over my head full of curly black hair. "Ain't no gel in my shit." I opened the overhead garage door of the shop, and the three of us went inside.

"Yeah, whatever, nigga. You got that soul glow shit up in there. Every time you get up off a sofa, it's a stain where ya head was and shit. That's how I be knowin' where you at all the time. I just follow the drip, nigga."

"You just mad 'cause ya nappy-head ass can't get bitches like this curly-head nigga get."

"Bitches love a nappy nigga, cuz. I make them feel safe. A curly-head nigga can't protect them, if need be. And they know that shit, too. That's why they only fuck with ya type long enough to get pregnant by you, so they baby can have that good shit, then they wind up marryin' a nigga like me."

"So that means I get the pussy and you get the commitment? That sound like a plan to me."

Brock put up his middle finger at me and then proceeded to get to work, cleaning and organizing the shop before it opened for business.

"Y'all niggas crazy," Kenny commented.

"That be that, nigga," I said. "But on another note, what's up? What happened with that situation?" I turned my attention completely to Kenny.

"Let's go in ya dad office," Kenny said.

"Cool, but we gotta hurry up 'fore that nigga get here. You know he don't be wantin' mafuckas in his office when he ain't here."

"Yeah, especially not me," Kenny said.

"So what happened? I see they let y'all out."

"Yeah, man, that was crazy. But they basically gave us all court dates. But you know me, I'm goin' have the top defense team in the city fightin' that shit. I'll beat the case. I ain't worried about that."

"That's what's up," I said, rubbing my goatee. "So what got you out the bed this early in the morning? I ain't seen you at the shop at this hour in years."

"I need a favor." Kenny's favorite words slid off his tongue.

I braced myself and then asked, "What's that?"

Kenny burst into laughter and then playfully hit me on my chest. "It ain't nothin' like that, nigga! Look at you gettin' all nervous and uptight now when I tell you I need a favor."

I laughed back but not as hard. "Naw, I just be waitin' to hear what you want a nigga to do now, that's all. You know how you get with ya favors. You never know what you goin' ask me to do."

"I know. I know. I do be comin' up with 'em, don't I? But naw, this is somethin' light."

"What's up?"

"Won't you ask ya pop to give my girl a gig?"

"Leah?" I asked.

"Yeah. She be buggin' about bein' bored and wantin' somethin' to do during the day. I figured I would ask y'all 'cause y'all like family, so it won't be no long, drawn-out application process. Plus, from what I saw today, y'all could use somebody here to open this bitch up on time, ya kna mean."

I didn't respond right away, and Kenny felt the need to fill the dead space.

"I mean, think about it. Ask ya pop. See what he say and get back with me, that's all."

"All right, yeah, I'll do that," I said, walking Kenny out of my dad's office and to the front door of the shop.

"Try to get him to do it, though," Kenny added as he walked over to his car. " 'Cause on top of everything, we could really use the extra money, even if it's just 'til we get enough for the retainer. Wouldn't wanna have to fight this case with a PD. Shit like that'll have niggas ready to tell on everybody just for a lighter sentence. Ya know what I'm talkin' 'bout?"

I couldn't help my eyebrows from bending as I deciphered what Kenny was saying. I hoped he wasn't insinuating that if I didn't get Leah a job, he would alert authorities that I had a part to play in that shit he got caught up in. I hoped he wasn't taking things to that level. I mean, granted, he looked out for me in the past, and I owed him for it. But I hated that he took advantage of that fact. And I knew he felt like as long as he had something to hold over my head, he could get me to do just about anything for him. But that wasn't the case, and I needed for him to know that before things got too out of hand. I needed to nip shit in the butt, and just as I was about to, he called himself, cleaning his shit up.

"Aww, nigga, I'm just fuckin' witchu." He laughed. "I wouldn't do no shit like that. But please get my girl a gig before she nag me to death."

I nodded. "I'm goin' see what I can do," I said, still feeling uneasy about the indirect threat he threw at me. He may have said he was joking, but knowing Kenny the way I did, it was no telling with that nigga. He could be a shady mothafucka sometimes.

Just as Kenny pulled out of his parking spot, my dad pulled in it. The loud roar of the Viper engine stopped abruptly as my dad turned off the ignition and hopped out the truck.

The first thing that came out my dad's mouth was, "What was that nigga here for?"

"Oh, Kenny?"

"Yeah. What he want?"

I followed my dad in the shop, walking fast to keep up with his pace. "He didn't want nothin' like that. He just wanted me to ask you could you give his girl a job."

"What? What I look like, givin' that nigga's girl a job? What I look like, givin' anybody he refer a job? So they can do what he did and jeopardize not only my business but my life! He must be smokin' dope!"

"I know. I thought the same thing. But the way he broke it down to me, it ain't like that," I said, beginning my attempt at trying to convince my dad otherwise.

"Yo, where's everybody at?" my dad asked as he walked into his office. "It's ten minutes to nine, and I ain't got no secretary here to answer them phones that's about to start ringing, no frame guy, no painter, not even a manager to manage the mafuckas if they was here! It look like I'm goin' be firing a whole lot of people today!" my dad snapped.

Then Brock called out from the floor, "I'm here, Vic!"

"Yeah, just my luck. The mafuckin' janitor the only mafucka on time in this bitch!"

I smirked at the insult and reminded myself to bust on Brock about it later. But now was the time to press my dad to give Leah a job. I mean, Kenny said he was joking about rattin' me out if I didn't pull strings for him on this, but I didn't believe his words. His body language said it all. So to protect me, I figured I had to get his girl a job. Besides, Leah was cool peoples. She wasn't the type to bring drama to the shop like my dad suspected. If anything, she could bring order.

"The thing is, Dad, Kenny's girl need to stack a couple dollars real quick. She got some loans or somethin' she gotta pay back," I lied. "He said she probably won't even be workin' here past a few months. Plus, we could use a good secretary, as you see. And if she could open the shop, that would help, too. That way I can be out chasin' during rush hour instead of havin' to be here to open up."

Brock butted in as he was emptying the trash can next to my dad's desk. "Yes, please get somebody else to open up, 'cause he be late every mornin' and I be freezin' my balls off."

"Janitors don't talk, they sweep," I teased Brock.

My dad sighed and said, "You vouch for this girl?"

"Yeah. She mess with Kenny, but she's not Kenny. You know what I mean?"

"Well, I'm goin' take ya word for it. But she's ya responsibility. I'm goin' need you to bring her up to speed. Even if you gotta leave the streets alone for a week or so to show her what has to be done here in the office, then that's what you do."

I nodded. "That's cool."

I started to walk out of my dad's office, and he stopped me.

"Nas."

I turned around. "Hah?"

"This decision better not come back to bite me in the ass."

I shook my head and said, "Naw. It won't."

I left the shop, got in my black Dodge Viper pickup truck—one of four that my dad bought for all his chasers to chase out of—and on my way to post up at Fifty-second and Spruce I called Kenny.

"Tell Leah she can start Monday," I said.

"That's what's up, homie. You always come through."

"Let's just make sure history don't repeat itself," I added.

"Oh naw, nigga. I ain't got eyes in the back of my head. I ain't worried about the past."

"Cool."

"All right."

" 'Bye."

Leah

I loaded up the dishwasher with the dirty dishes Kenny managed to fill up the sink with while I was in jail, folded the last load of clothes, swept and mopped the floors, dusted off everything, and lit a few candles. *I live in a multimillion-dollar home and don't have a housekeeper,* I thought. That's some ghetto shit. The last thing on my list was ordering Cajun Chicken Chesapeake for six from Bourbon Blue. Kenny would pick it up on his way in.

I was finished with everything by seven, giving me just enough time to shower and change out of my tights and oversized T-shirt and into a pair of sweats before Kenny's company arrived at eight. He was having a meeting with his accountant and his top workers to discuss his finances and opportunities for him to merge out of the drug game and into legit business.

Usually when Kenny had meetings at the house, I would find something to do to occupy my time, which often was shopping or going to visit my mom. But this time I felt obligated to sit in on the meeting. As much as I was having second thoughts about it, I had a deal with the police, and my freedom from both jail and Kenny depended on my keeping it. So I needed to start gathering information, and what better time than at the meeting.

I heard Kenny pull up in the garage, and I greeted him at the door.

"You smell good," he said as I hugged him.

"Thank you. So does that food," I said, relieving Kenny of one of the bags.

I immediately started taking the containers of food out of the bags and placing everything on one big tray on the counter. I took out my Wedgwood china and the Waterford glasses. I laid out jeweled wood place mats and started setting the dining room table—half of it anyway. We didn't need twelve settings, and to make it appear more intimate, I removed the six additional chairs we would not be using. I lifted the heavy custom wooden chairs and placed them in the adjacent study. Then I rearranged the remaining six chairs, putting three on each side of the table. That way no one person would be too far away from anyone else and there was plenty of elbow room for everyone to eat comfortably.

In the meantime Kenny freshened up. The doorbell rang just as Kenny was coming back downstairs. The guests arrived all at once, having riden together in one car, except Sammy, Kenny's accountant, who had driven himself.

"Hey, Sammy." I greeted him with a hug as he came in. We exchanged kisses on the cheek, and I took his tan trench coat and plaid scarf and hung them in the coat closet in the foyer.

Behind Sammy was Sky, Kenny's transporter. Basically, he was responsible for taking drugs down South and returning with money. I greeted him the same way—a hug, a kiss—and I took his coat. Next was Raj, Kenny's best friend and right-hand man. He pretty much helped Kenny manage all his street hustlers or corner boys. Last in was Tim, Kenny's older brother and his muscle. As a result of his frequent stints in the penitentiary, he was real buff, so his appearance alone was threatening. And he had a reputation for being ruthless and for torturing niggas. I wasn't as enthusiastic when I greeted him as I was when I greeted the others. I never had good vibes about Tim. He rubbed me the wrong way. Maybe it was his cold, standoffish demeanor. I didn't know. But I felt extremely intimidated by him.

Everybody sat at the table, and I served them dinner while they began their meeting. I must say I was being extra hospitable. I didn't know if it was my nerves or what.

"All right, I'm goin' get straight to the point, Sammy. Where the fuck is all my money goin'?" Kenny started.

"It's all documented," Sammy said, punching keys on his laptop. "Well, with you refinancing everybody's houses recently your mortgage payments have gone up—"

"How much?" Kenny asked.

I tuned in myself to hear the answer. I never knew how much Kenny was paying for everybody's mortgage. Quite frankly, I didn't think he should have been paying anybody's mortgage but ours. Every nigga sittin' at this table made enough money to pay his own.

"Let's see," Sammy said, calling up more information on his computer. "Yours is now eighteen thousand six hundred sixty-nine dollars a month; your brother's is now nine thousand three hundred and thirty-four a month; Roger's and Sky's are each seven thousand two hundred and twenty-three."

"Shit, nigga, you pay more in mortgages than what my pop make in a year," Raj said, seemingly proud. "How many niggas you know that's under age thirty that can do that shit. We up, niggas!"

"You all are doing well, yes, but I don't know if I would celebrate right now," Sammy said. "You see, Kenny, your monthly bills are at seventy-three thousand. And for the last six months you've only been bringin' in on average fifty to sixty thousand. In addition, there's been a lot of sporadic spending over that time period, causing you to fall behind."

"That's fuckin' ridiculous, though, Sammy. Why wouldn't you give me the heads-up that I'm headin' for broke before I actually get there? I mean, ain't that what I pay you for?" Kenny addressed Sammy as he chomped on a forkful of pasta.

Fumbling to adjust his glasses on his face, Sammy answered, "Well, you're not broke at all. You're just digging into your reserves at this point. And I actually called this meeting tonight to give you the heads-up on things."

"Okay, so what do I have in reserve?"

"You haaaave . . ." Sammy stretched his words as he punched more keys on his laptop. "You have two point seven million as of right now. That's down from three point one six months ago."

Kenny mumbled some figures and calculations then said, "So you sayin' I spent four hundred grand in six months, in addition to my monthly bills?"

"I'm afraid so."

The looks on a few of Kenny's partners' faces told me that I wasn't the only one shocked by the accountant's report of Kenny's outlandish spending. I started adding stuff up in my head, trying to figure out what he had spent so much money on. Okay, granted, he treated himself to the Maserati for his twenty-fifth birthday a few months ago. That was a hundred thousand. Then there was the forty days we spent at our marina house in the Turks and Caicos for the holidays. That was probably about a hundred and fifty grand, most of which went to the yacht he chartered. Okay, so that was a little more than half the money, but the other portion I couldn't account for, and I couldn't help but wonder how much of it went to other girls.

"Somethin' gotta give, man. I can't keep blowin' money like this," Kenny stated.

The mood in the room grew somber. Niggas was probably scared that Kenny was goin' to announce that he was goin' to have to put the brakes on payin' all their mortgages.

But offering hope, Sammy put his finger up and said, "That's another reason why I called this meeting tonight. I wanted to propose something to you all."

Everybody turned to look at Sammy.

"I think you all need to consider investing, particularly in real estate. With the housing market in the sewer, it's a good time to buy rental properties. People are losing their homes and can't afford mortgages, but still they need a place to live. And I was just introduced to an amazing opportunity that I want to bring to you all. One of my business partner's golf buddies is liquidating a lot of his income-producing properties. He has a package of mobile-home parks for sale . . ."

I looked at everybody's reactions to Sammy's proposal that they buy trailer parks, and, as I expected, none of them seemed interested, except for Kenny. Kenny showed interest in any ideas that led to making money—big or small.

"I know it doesn't sound as glamorous as, say, an apartment building or condo conversions, but when you do the math, it has the potential to make more money than any of that other stuff that's on the market right now. He has five mobile parks that he's getting rid of for a good price, and they bring in substantial monthly income already, but that's with the tenants occupying them at beneath-market rates. So if you put a little bit of money into them, update them some, you could raise rents and just about triple the net worth."

A few eyebrows raised. I imagined there were dollar signs floating around in everybody's heads.

Sammy went on, "The bottom line is, you all need to start making your money make money. And I know it's hard because you do what you do and are trying to stay undetected as far as your assets go, but there are ways to have paper trails that are perfectly legal."

"You talkin' washin' the money?" Tim asked.

Sammy nodded. "Yeah, basically."

"Money launderin'," Kenny mumbled, wiping his mouth with a folded napkin.

"I don't know about that," Raj spoke up.

"Yeah, I know, 'cause that shit can catch you up, too. Look at what happened with Irv Gotti and them," Sky said.

Then Sammy interjected, "It's definitely not a hundred percent foolproof. Consider it like a condom. It's ninety-nine percent effective. The thing is, you can't put your money behind mega superstars or big businesses that are already on the radar. You have to put it behind small ventures, low-key things that won't raise any eyebrows or attract a lot of attention, and with the economy being in shambles right now, there are plenty small businesses that would be willing to launder your money in exchange for financial support."

Kenny glanced over at me. "That's why all them niggas be buyin' their girls' hair salons and shit. Leah, you want a hair salon?"

Hell, yeah, I thought. Anything to put me in position to make my own money, but before I could say anything Sammy butted in, "No, that's not smart either. Not right now. You don't wanna put your money into something that you're attached to. Then the question of where the money generated from still gets asked. You have to find a business that already exists and make a deal with the owner. And, of course, make sure it's somebody you can trust."

"And somebody you can get at easily, in case for some reason he end up being untrustworthy," Sky added.

"The point is, once you find the business you feel comfortable with, make the owner put you on the payroll. They will start issuing you checks; you'll really be being paid out of your own money, but it will look like it's coming out of their business account instead of from the streets."

Kenny nodded and seemed to be in deep thought.

"This way, you all can start using the so-called money you make from your employer"—Sammy made quotation marks with his fingers—"to put in banks and build capital, and then you can start funneling it into other things like the real estate deal I'm proposing . . ."

Kenny sipped his water and asked, "But will homie be willing to hold off selling the package until I clean up enough money to get them? That might take a minute."

"Well, right now he's willing to do owner financing, which means he will keep the properties in his name and set it up with you so you will give him a monthly payment based on the amount you would finance to buy the properties."

"You lost me," Kenny said.

"It would be as if he was the bank giving you the loan," I jumped in to clarify it for Kenny.

"Exactly," Sammy said. "He's willing to do that for a year, which is plenty of time to clean up enough cash."

Kenny nodded and said, " I like that idea. I think I can make that happen."

Then the other guys nodded in agreement. I swore they were a bunch of yes sirs. If Kenny liked it, they loved it. But who was I to talk? I was in the same boat as them. I needed Kenny financially like they did, maybe even more. So just like them, I tended to go along with whatever he said.

"That could work," I volunteered my opinion as I looked at Kenny.

"That's the only way you're gonna see real growth, when your money is moving around. When it stays still in a safe or under a mattress, it starts to deplete. And if you put it in the bank, it can get frozen the minute you become the target of an investigation."

"Speakin' of which," Raj said, looking at Kenny, "what the hell happened? Fuck they lock you up on?"

Aww shit, I thought. Why did this conversation have to come up? The last thing I needed was for the question to arise about how we all got out without penalty. I didn't know if my nerves could handle lying to all of them, especially that damn Tim. He was good at reading people, and I didn't want him to get any ideas about me. He was the type of person who would dig and dig and dig until he found a loophole in a nigga's story. I felt myself tensing up.

"Aww, man," Kenny began, "I was buggin' out for a minute, feelin' like I was losing everything. Wound up stagin' a accident to hustle up a couple dollars, and the corner I did it on was being surveilled by the mothafuckin' police," Kenny explained, almost as if he was bragging.

Everybody laughed except Tim, who maintained a serious expression. I myself chuckled. Then I stood and started gathering dishes and eating utensils to remove them from the table. I figured my action would give the hint that the meeting was over.

"This nigga got over two million in the stash, and he chasin' car insurance claims for a few thousand dollars," Tim commented.

"It's easy money, nigga, and it's quick. And I know that shit like the back of my hand, plus I got people who can help me pull it off, so that's why I dibble in it ever so often." Kenny paused and looked up at me as I gathered dishes. I felt him looking at me, and I shot him a quick smile. "But not no more. I'm cool on all that now. I ain't tryna put my girl in a position like that again. Plus, the money ain't worth the headache."

"I don't see why you thought it was worth it to begin with, brah. If you needed a few thousand, what was wrong with diggin' in ya stash?"

Kenny jumped to his own defense, "Naw see, I got a system. I give Sammy money every month, and he go 'head and pay all my bills. If it's ever short, he got permission to take it out of my reserves. Then I keep a stash for myself, for my pocket. And I started noticin' my pocket money dwindling. And I don't wanna stop givin' Sammy what I'm givin' him for my bills, 'cause then he goin' dig more and more into my reserves, and once that's gone, I'm cracked, havin' to start over from the bottom. So whenever I see my pocket money gettin' low, that's when I start scramblin' around tryin' to hustle some money up real quick," Kenny explained.

"Well, if that's ya system, you need a new one. We built up too much to let it all crumble over small change. You should be tryin' to stay as far away from the precinct as possible. All it take is for you to get locked up with the wrong mafucka. They get to talkin', and ya ass is done."

Tim's words sent chills through me.

"That's true." Raj sighed.

"Well, that's one thing I ain't gotta worry about. I keep thorough niggas around me, and I only do dirt with niggas who I can trust, like my baby," Kenny said, grabbing hold of my waist as I stood beside his chair with dishes in my hands. "She took the charge for me," Kenny lied.

For once, I was relieved that he didn't tell the truth. I mean, I didn't expect him to tell his group of criminal friends that his girl made a deal with the cops and became a snitch to get us all off. But then again, you never knew with Kenny. He liked to brag so much that sometimes he bragged about the wrong things to the wrong people. I was glad that this wasn't one of those times. I could imagine Tim interrogating me about it and then puttin' it in Kenny's head to watch out for me. I could imagine him saying something like, If she'll rat on one nigga, she'll rat on them all.

"Word?" Raj questioned, seemingly impressed.

"Wow," Sammy uttered.

They all looked at me, including Tim. What were they expecting my reaction to be? I wondered. Was I supposed to be upset or content? Well, from how Kenny put it out there, like it was a good thing, I decided to give a half grin.

"And I owe her big-time for it, too. You can't get most niggas to do no shit like that for you these days."

"Fuck no," Sky said.

"Naw, you can't," Tim added. "You got you somethin' special." He sized me up as he picked his teeth with a toothpick he'd apparently brought with him to the dinner meeting.

"Plus," Kenny continued, "if mafuckas know one thing, they know not to turn on me. I'd like to think that I put in enough work on the streets to make that clear by now, kna mean?"

"You never know, though," Tim persisted. "Just chill on the extra shit, that's all."

"I am. I ain't tryna keep duckin' the law," Kenny said. "That's why my man Sammy is here tonight. He goin' help me put my money in the right place so I can walk away from the game before my time run out."

"So does that mean it's a yes? You want to move forward on the mobile-park deal?" Sammy took the opportunity to get back on topic. And I was so grateful he did. I didn't know how much more my nerves could take talking about our arrest.

"Yeah, let's do it," Kenny concluded.

"Great. I'll call you in the morning to get started on some paperwork."

At that, Sammy closed up his laptop and put it in its bag. He excused himself from the meeting. I walked him to the door, retrieved his coat and scarf, and saw him out.

The guys spent a few more minutes talking about what was going on in the streets and in their trade, and then they ended their meeting.

It was a quarter to eleven by the time they left. I had unloaded the clean dishes and put them away and was reloading the dishwasher with the dirty ones we had just used when Kenny came into the kitchen.

"What did you think about that meeting?" Kenny asked me.

"Interesting," I said, shrugging my shoulders.

"Yeah? You ain't never sit in on one of them before."

"I know. I was goin' to go to Saks since I had got a text message from Walter, the guy who always help me when I'm there, tellin' me that they had some new Chanel shoes come in in my size," I lied.

"Why you ain't go?" Kenny probed.

"By the time I finished cleaning this damn house, they were closed."

"Yeah, well, I'm glad you was able to be here for this one, anyway, 'cause I'm goin' need you to help me wash my money."

"How?" I quizzed.

"Well, for starters, you goin' be workin' down at the shop come Monday," Kenny informed me.

"Huh?" I was confused.

"I got you a job at Vic's."

I didn't say anything, but my face still read confused.

Kenny elaborated, "How else are you supposed to get information for the po-po? That *was* the deal you worked out, right?"

I nodded.

"All right then. So anyway, once you get in good a little bit, I'm goin' need you to have all them niggas in there givin' you they checks in exchange for cash. I'm goin' use them to clean up my money."

I nodded again. "Okay," I nonchalantly agreed, then turned my attention back to the dishes.

I felt Kenny staring at me for a little while before he disappeared from the kitchen. My nerves were shot. It seemed like Kenny was testing me. Like he knew I was up to something by sitting in on his meeting. And to top things off, he took it upon himself to get me a job at the shop, like that was his way of making sure I was telling the truth about the deal I'd made with the police. Kenny was no dummy, and as I finished cleaning up, I wondered if he was on to me already. A part of me believed so, but another part thought he was just baiting me. Either way, I had put myself in a situation from which there was no turning back. So my only choice was to play it all the way out to the end.

Nasir

This was the first day I had got up out the bed without pressing Snooze on the alarm clock since I'd been assigned to opening the shop for my dad. He used to have the manager open and close the shop, but after he lost the keys for the fifth time, my dad asked me to do it until he found someone more responsible.

I jumped in the shower, and, instead of throwing on some jeans, a long-john shirt, and Timbs, like I normally did, I put on a navy-blue-and-white D&G hoodie and some D&G high-top sneakers. I sprayed some Creed cologne on me, and even went in my watch box and put on one of my Rolexes. Even though Leah wasn't my girl, I felt the need to impress her. And it wasn't on no shady shit, either, because I wasn't the type to mess with my homie's girl. Plus, I had a girl myself. It was just something about women, period, that made me want to clean up for them. At least that's what I was telling myself.

I walked out of my apartment and took the elevator down to the lobby. I dropped my nineteen-hundred-fifty-dollar rent check in the box near the mail room. I had to pay an extra fifty dollars because it was late. It wasn't that I didn't have the money to pay it, it was just that I had been workin' so much, pulling a lot of all-nighters, that I forgot about it. And it wasn't like I got a bill in the mail reminding me about it. Plus, I was in no hurry to pay nineteen hundred for a place that I didn't own. And every time I thought about that, I told myself that I needed to start lookin' into gettin' a house. But the only thing that kept me from doing that was Tara, the girl I had been messin' with for the past year.

Her lease was almost up on her apartment, and she'd been hintin' around to me that we should get a house together. I was feelin' her and everything, and we'd had a pretty good relationship, but I was cool on gettin' a crib with her. I mean, I always told myself that I would wait 'til I was thirty before I settled down with a chick. So technically I had five and a half more years left for that. But I did tell Tara that if she kept playin' her cards right, she might be able to get me to do it in three.

Real talk though, I did want to get my own crib and well before three years. I just didn't feel like hearin' Tara's mouth if I did. *Why don't you want a house with me? You do plan on havin' a future with me, right? You been livin' on your own since you were nineteen, I'm sure you've had plenty of time to see what it was like. What, do you have something to hide?* Just thinking about it gave me a headache, so fuck it, rent it was.

"Good morning, Mr. Freeman," the doorman greeted me as I was on my way out of my building.

"What's up, Ed?"

"Just tryna keep warm, that's all," he said.

"I hear that," I said. "Have a good one."

I walked outside, and Ed's words had meaning. The January cold smacked me in the face, then seemed to wrap itself around my body as I walked to my truck, parked in my reserved spot.

I drove to the shop, which was only a twenty-minute commute from my apartment in Manayunk. And although a short distance, somehow I was always late getting there, no matter how early I left. However, that morning was different. I got to the shop at seven forty-five, fifteen minutes early, even after first stopping at Dunkin' Donuts. And the one day I had my ass there early, Brock wasn't there to witness it.

I opened the overhead door and walked in the shop, then I unlocked my dad's office. I turned on all the lights and the heat. The shop was so big, it would take every bit of an hour to warm it up. In thinking about that, I felt proud. My dad had started as a chaser like me and ended up opening and operating one of the largest body shops in the city. I respected my dad for his ability to do that and even more so for being in business for almost eight years. That was unheard of where I came from. Most businesses fail within the first five years, let alone black-owned businesses. Where I was from, black people closed their businesses just as fast as they opened them. So I really looked up to my dad as a business owner. He was the exception to the rule.

It started to warm up, so I took off my leather Polo coat and hung it in a locked closet in my dad's office. I got comfortable, eager to start the workday. I organized the desk that sat diagonal from my dad's; that's where we'd put Leah. I was in the midst of making copies of claim forms when I heard Leah's voice.

"Hellooo," she sang.

I got up out my dad's chair and walked out onto the floor.

"What's up, Leah?" I greeted her. She gave me a warm smile as she walked over to me.

I hadn't seen Leah since the night she and Kenny got locked up, and it had been dark and she was at a distance, so I didn't get a good look at her then. Before that, it had been a few months since I'd seen her. I almost forgot how bad she was. She had a body like Meagan Good's, petite with big boobs. Her face was exotic-looking, like a black Kim Kardashian, and she had this sweet, innocent charm about her that reminded me of Lauren London.

Her long hair lay like silk on top of her short black mink. She had on black skinny jeans that stopped right at the top of a pair of black-and-gold Chanel shoes. When she took off her coat, I couldn't help but notice her breasts as they pressed against her silky gold blouse. She had these gold bangles on her arm that grabbed my attention when she held her coat out to me.

"Where should I put this?" she asked.

I reached out and grabbed it. "I'll lock it in my dad's closet for you."

"Thanks," she said, rubbing her hands together. "So, where's ev-erybody? Or am I that early?"

I turned to go back in my dad's office to put Leah's coat up. In that time, I forced my mind off the fact that Leah was a perfect ten and on to the fact that I had a girl whom I supposedly loved.

"They should be walkin' in here any minute. Everybody usually gets here between eight and eight thirty," I told Leah. And as hard as I was trying to avoid looking at her, the sparkle from the gold-and-diamond Rolex she glanced at on her wrist brought my eyes back to her.

"Oh, okay, so I guess the games will begin within the next twenty minutes."

"Well, actually," I said, hanging up Leah's coat, which smelled of a sweet fragrance, "I wanted to start showing you some stuff now."

Leah's eyes lit up. "You're gonna be training me?"

"Yeah. Why you ask like that? You don't think I can?"

"No, no. It's not that. I'm just relieved. I mean, I know you, so I feel comfortable making mistakes around you. If it were somebody else, I would be nervous."

"Oh. Well, it's nothing to be nervous about. It's a pretty easygoing position. And once you get the hang of it, it'll be nothin'."

"I just haven't had a job in so long," Leah said.

"Well I'm sure it's like ridin' a bike." I pulled Leah's chair out and gestured for her to sit down.

Still wearing a smile, she did. I began to explain her duties to her.

"Basically, your job will be to answer the phones and handle the customers who come to set up claims. And what that means is, they were in an accident and they have to call their insurance company to report it. They'll get a claim number, and you'll put it in their file, along with their contact information and their signature, giving us permission to fix their car . . ."

"O-kay," Leah sang, as if I was giving her too much to take in at once.

Taking the hint, I assured her, "It's not as confusing as it sounds. You'll catch on." Then I continued, "When you answer the phone, you say, 'Hello, Alliance Collision. How may I help you?' You know, professional."

Leah nodded.

"For now until you learn the business, just take messages. Most people will call to check the status of their car. They're on a whiteboard that hangs on the wall out on the floor. For instance, it'll say somethin' like '2006 blue Maxima waiting for adjuster' or '2007 white Pathfinder parts have been ordered'—stuff like that. If a car isn't listed on there, just ask someone on the floor for a status. If no one knows, ask my dad. But my dad should be a last resort. If he's not here, just tell the customer you will find out and give them a call back."

"Okay." Leah nodded.

"Other calls will be from adjusters wanting to come out and inspect cars. All you gotta do is take the date and time he'll be out and put it in the customer's file."

"And the adjuster is the person who works for the insurance company who comes out and writes estimates, right?"

"Yeah."

CHASER

"Okay, I do remember some of these terms from when Kenny used to chase."

"I told you, it's like ridin' a bike."

Leah smiled, and I smiled back. Then I proceeded to give her the business. "If you get a call from a customer wanting to pull their car—"

"Wait a minute," Leah said. "What do you mean, 'pull their car'?"

"Oh, that just means they want to come get their car from here and get it fixed somewhere else."

"Oh, okay."

"Just give the call to my dad. If he can't convince them to keep the car here, then he'll give you a list of charges. Then you'll get back on the phone and tell them what it's goin' cost for them to get their car. The last important thing you'll probably handle on the phone is callin' insurance companies and having them send the checks here."

"What do you mean?"

"After the estimate is written and the work is pretty much done on the car, the insurance company sends a check that covers the estimate to the customer or their insured. But sometimes the customer will keep the check and we lose money fixing their car."

"How can the customer keep the check? Then they won't get their car back, right?"

"Naw, they won't get their car back, but some of them don't care. They see that money and get greedy. So it's best for us if the insurance company either sends the check straight to us or makes it payable to us along with their insured."

"Okay. I understand that."

I started showing Leah the forms that go in new customers' files when Brock walked in.

"It must be as cold in hell as it is outside! This nigga not only here, but he's workin' and it's not even nine o'clock yet!" Brock exclaimed, making sure to stomp the snow off his boots before walking in my dad's office.

"Naw, hell ain't goin' see a cold day unless you come in here without talkin' shit," I shot back.

"And you dope-boy fresh, too? Fuck cold, the devil down there mafucka ice skatin', I'm sure!"

Leah glanced at me and then at Brock.

"Oh, I'm sorry, Leah," Brock said. "I don't usually talk that way around women, but Nasir caught me off guard. He ain't the most punctual mafucka. And he damn sure don't be smellin' good."

Leah chuckled.

"Ain't it a filled-up trash can around here with ya name on it?"

"Yeah, and I'm goin' get to it, too, soon as I finish with the Newport that also got my name on it." Brock took a pack of cigarettes from his back pocket as he started walking out of my dad's office. "The power of the p.u.s.s.y," he sang under his breath.

"You gotta excuse that nigga," I told Leah. "His mom was smokin' while she was pregnant with 'im."

Leah chuckled and said, "Y'all funny. Working might not end up being so bad."

I chuckled with her and started to ask what she meant by her last comment. I mean, I thought she wanted to work. I thought that was why Kenny came down here askin' me to put her on. But I brushed it off as the shop started to fill up with workers—my dad being among them.

"What's up, Nas?" My dad stopped to shake my hand before reaching his desk.

"What's up, Dad?"

"What's up, babe?" my dad then greeted Leah.

"Good morning," she said.

"So you're our new secretary?"

"Yes, I am."

"Well, hopefully you can bring some order to this place," my dad said. "Is Nasir takin' it easy on you? He's not movin' too fast, is he?"

"No, he's movin' at a good pace," Leah replied, glancing up at me with that pretty smile of hers. Our eyes locked on each other's for a moment, as if we were in a trance. Then we both snapped out of it and turned our attention back to work.

My dad took a few calls, made his rounds, and collected whatever checks had come in the mail over the weekend, and he left. Meanwhile, I continued to show Leah everything she needed to know. I helped her deal with a couple customers who called or came in. I even got to show her how to set up a claim. She did all right, too. Overall, the day went pretty good—fast, too. I expected it to be long and boring sitting at a desk, but it wasn't. Between Brock and his jokes and Leah's company, I didn't feel frustrated like I usually felt when my dad asked me to do something other than going out in my truck chasing. In fact, it felt good not to be cooped up in the truck, listening to the nonstop crackling and beeping of the scanners. And being in the warm shop definitely beat freezin' my ass off at a hit. Don't get me wrong, I could never get used to the nine-to-five office routine, but for that one week I had to train Leah, I looked forward to it.

Tuesday through Thursday went a lot like Monday. I got to the shop early enough to heat it, light it, and make it comfortable for Leah. I walked her through calls and claims and even got the chance to show her the procedure for when a car is released. And at the end of the day I'd lock up the shop, see Leah to her Jaguar CXF, and go my way. But Friday was different—not in terms of it being a payday and the start of the weekend, but in terms of how it ended for Leah and me.

I closed and locked my dad's office door. Then, after walking out of the shop, I pressed the Lock button on the garage-door opener. As the overhead door dropped to a close, I looked around and noticed I didn't see Leah's car.

"Where did you park today?" I asked, planning to see her to her car.

"I didn't drive today. Kenny dropped me off."

"Oh. So he's pickin' you up?"

"Yeah. We made plans to go out straight from here, and we didn't want to have to take two cars," she explained.

"Oh, that's what's up," I said, concluding that was the reason Leah was dressed extra nice that day. She looked good every day, but that day she went hard. She had on a gray fitted skirt that went to her knees and had a small split up the back. Tucked in it was a white blouse that clung to her stomach and breasts but was loose in the sleeves. A few Chanel pearls fell onto her cleavage. And her hair was up in a sexy ponytail. She had on some ankle boots with a high heel that put definition in her calves every time she took a step. And instead of her black mink she wore a chinchilla wrap.

"Yeah," she put on a half smile. "It's our anniversary."

"Oh, okay," I said.

"You don't have to wait," she said.

"I know. But it's cool. I don't wanna leave you out here by yourself."

"Yeah, but I don't want you to be standin' out here in the cold," she said.

"I'm a man. I can take a little bit of cold. And if it get too bad, I'm goin' open the shop back up."

"All right. If you say so." Then she took her cell phone from her pocketbook and dialed somebody. I assumed Kenny. She held it to her ear for a while, then took it away and repeated the process. After three times, she put the phone back in her pocketbook.

"You want me to open the shop?" I asked, sensing that either the blistery weather or those high-ass shoes were causing her discomfort.

Before she could answer, she started digging around in her pocketbook, trying to locate her ringing phone.

"Hello," Leah said into the phone. She paused. "I'm out here waiting on you. Where are you?"

CHASER

I looked down the street.

"Well, when *will* you be here? It's freezin' out here!" Leah ranted. "Forty-five minutes?"

I glanced over at her.

Then she said, "You know what, forget it! I'll catch a cab. Just meet me at the house!" Leah pressed the End button on her phone and threw it in her pocketbook. It was clear she was angry.

"I can take you home if you want me to," I offered.

"No, you don't have to. I'm just goin' call a cab. But if you could open the shop for me so I can wait inside, I would appreciate it."

"I would, but I don't know how long a cab goin' be, and I do have plans myself, so it'll be better for me to drop you off at your house."

She sighed. "I don't wanna inconvenience you, so whatever is best."

I walked to my truck and opened the passenger door for Leah to get in. I started it up and immediately turned on the seat heaters. I let the engine run for a good five minutes before I turned on the heat. Having Leah in my truck had my hormones goin' crazy. I started having all these thoughts about what it would be like to lay her down in the backseat and tear that ass up. She was pissed off at Kenny, too. I might have had a chance.

But, naw, I wasn't goin' take advantage of her situation with her dude. I just kept my feelings at bay. There would be a next time, I thought. I knew Kenny. He was one of those no-good-ass niggas. I was sure there would come a time where he would make Leah mad again, and I would be there for her then, like I was there for her now.

And don't get me wrong. I wasn't tryin' to step on Kenny's toes. But he was leavin' me with no choice. Besides, it wasn't like he ain't never stepped on my toes.

"Where y'all stayin' at now?" I asked Leah as I put the truck in drive.

"Across City Line Avenue," she said, buckling her seat belt.

I pulled off and headed toward City Line. Once there, Leah guided me the rest of the way to Kenny's and her mini-mansion in Bryn Mawr, a wealthy suburb outside Philly. It was only about twenty-five minutes from the shop, but it was a whole different world when comparing the two neighborhoods.

"Thank you so much, Nasir," Leah said, turning to me.

"No problem. I wasn't goin' make you take a cab, and I damn sure wasn't goin' leave you stranded."

"You was always the sweet one," she said.

"What you mean?"

"Nothing," she said, shaking her head and opening the door. "I don't wanna take up too much of your time. I know you got plans and all."

She got out and started the brief walk to her front door. Before she could get there I rolled down the window.

"Ay!" I called out to her.

She turned around.

"I don't really have plans tonight. I just said that so I could be the one to drop you off instead of a cab."

She smirked and said, "That's what I mean." Then she waved good-bye and continued to her door.

I rolled the window back up and drove off. The whole ride home, I thought about that girl. I imagined her being mine. And call me what you want, but if I was goin' move in a house with anybody, it would be Leah. And damn, I felt bad for having strong feelings like that for Leah and not for my own girl. But I couldn't help it. Leah did somethin' for me that no other girl has. And that was something I always felt.

Leah

I was sitting in the theater room eating a bowl of Frosted Flakes and watching *Family Feud* on the 102-inch projection screen. My intention when I first went in there was to put on a movie, but when I turned on the TV and saw that one of my favorite game shows was on, I couldn't resist. I had on my most comfortable pajamas, which were also my oldest pair, some blue flannel pants and a matching shirt that buttoned up, leaving everything to the imagination. I wanted to make it clear that Kenny wasn't getting any that night. I was hot with him. We had had seven o'clock reservations at Le Bec-Fin, and here it was nine and he wasn't even home yet.

"Shoes," I blurted out right after the *Family Feud* host read the question. Number one answer, like I thought. What else would a husband say his wife spent too much money on?

I ate the last spoonful of my cereal and then tipped the bowl up to my mouth and drank the milk. It wasn't the rack of lamb that my mouth watered for, but it curbed my appetite. That damn Kenny.

I got up to put my bowl in the dishwasher, and I heard the garage door opening. My heart started to race with anticipation. Should I curse him out and show him just how very pissed off I was at him for standing me up, or should I ignore him and act like it didn't faze me? I wanted to go with the former, but I had to wait and see what kind of mood he was in. If he came in actin' shitty, then I'd be better off ignoring him, leaving it alone. If he came in apologetic, though, I would be able to get away with letting him know how I felt.

"Baby, I'm so sorry," he apologized as soon as he walked in the door.

"Where were you?" I asked him, frustration in my tone. I looked down at the four Sneaker Villa bags he had in his hands, and I snapped, "I know you didn't stand me up to go shopping!"

"Of course not," he said, putting the bags down on the table. "I just got caught up. But I'm goin' make it up to you."

Normally I would not have pried. I would have let Kenny's answer be what it was. But I took that as an opportunity to get information out of him.

"Make it up to me how, Kenny? I got all dressed up, waited outside the shop in the cold for you, and missed the private dinner I had set up for us at Le Bec-Fin. How can you make up for that?"

"You right. It's goin' be hard to make that up. But what you want me to tell you? Some shit came up on me unexpected, and it kept me longer than I thought it would," Kenny explained vaguely as he opened the refrigerator and stood in front of it.

"What I want you to tell me?" I didn't let up. "I want you to tell me what exactly kept you from spending our three-year anniversary with me?"

Kenny closed the refrigerator and turned to look at me. Frowning, he asked, "What's with all the questions lately? What's this new you about? I said I got caught up! Why is this conversation goin' past that?"

"Because I'm tired, Kenny! I'm tired of sittin' back and lettin' you come, go, and do as you please, and not considering my feelings in the process."

"Not considerin' ya feelings! What the fuck you think I'm hustlin' my ass off for? I don't need a six-bedroom house, chinchillas, Jaguars, and shit! I don't need all this! This shit is for you! You the one cried to me that you couldn't stand livin' in that crampy two-bedroom apartment with ya mom, sharin' a room with ya alcoholic sister! Remember that? Now, I take you out of that situation, and you bitch and complain when I miss a fuckin' dinner date!"

"You know what, Kenny, go 'head and throw that in my face! But you and I both know that you ain't miss our dinner date because you were out hustlin'!"

"Aww, here we go," Kenny mumbled.

"And if I would've known that I was goin' be more miserable in this six-bedroom than I ever was in my mom's two-bedroom, trust me, I would've stayed put!"

"Bitch!" Kenny shouted as he slapped me across the mouth. "I'm dodgin' bullets tryin' to give you a better life, and this is how you talk to me?"

I stood stiff, holding my hand over my lip. I could tell it was busted. I didn't feel the need to say anything else because I had gotten Kenny where I wanted him. He snatched the Sneaker Villa bags off the table, held them upside down, and shook them until sneaker boxes fell to the floor. Along with the boxes fell brick-sized packages of a white powdery substance that I presumed to be cocaine.

Picking up one of the bricks, Kenny yelled, "This ain't hustlin'? Huh? This ain't what I was out doin' when I missed Le Fec Bec Fin, whatever the fuck!"

I remained stiff as I lowered my eyes, counting the number of bricks in my head.

"Now you owe me a fuckin' apology," Kenny said in a calmer tone. "Go in the bathroom and wash that blood off ya lip. Then come back in here and suck this anger up out me." He began unbuckling his belt as I walked to the powder room. I stared at myself in the mirror while dabbing my lip with a wet paper towel. I fought so hard to hold back tears that I ended up laughing. Then like a crazy woman I started talking to myself under my breath.

"You wasn't out grindin', nigga! I seen those Sneaker Villa bags over a week ago! Matter of fact, it was the night we staged that accident! And you goin' bring them in from the garage to cover up ya dirt! I know you was with a bitch!"

I threw the paper towel in the trash and walked back into the living room. Kenny was positioned on the couch with his pants down just under his butt. I dragged my feet getting over to him.

"Come on now," he said.

I got on my knees in front of him. Putting him in my mouth, I shut my eyes. As his dick filled the space in my mouth and his hand forced my head up and down, I couldn't help but wonder whose seconds I was getting—and on our anniversary of all days. *Kenny, you son of a bitch,* I thought, *every dog gets his day.*

Nasir

M"*edic Nine, Six-one and Chestnut.*" I jumped up out of my sleep and sat up in the driver's seat. I listened intently to the next words to come out of the dispatcher's mouth. My foot was already on the gas and gear shifted to drive. All I needed to hear was . . .

"*Injuries from an accident.*"

Skirrrrrrrt, I pulled out of the gas station parking lot like I was in a race car. My tow truck skidded up Spruce Street, disrupting the peace for sure. I got to a red light and stopped. But when I noticed out my side mirror that another tow truck was fast approaching, I put my foot back on the gas and ran through the light without hesitation.

The other tow truck followed right behind me, riding my ass, trying to get in front of me. I wasn't letting it happen, though. At the next red light, the same thing—I ran right through it. The chaser behind me didn't give up. He was still on my ass.

A line of early-morning rush-hour traffic was ahead of us, and it was a race to the front. I had two options: drive in the lane that was reserved for traffic going in the opposite direction and risk a head-on collision, or drive up on the curb and take the pavement to the light. I had to think fast because my competitor was right there on me.

I quickly looked around, getting a glimpse of everything that surrounded me—pedestrians, traffic, and the green light ahead that caused a flow of traffic to pour in the lane to my left, which I was considering taking. *The pavement it is,* I thought, as I jumped my truck on the curb and rode it to the intersection, where I was able to make a right turn off the busy street.

At that point my competitor was no longer in my rearview. I guessed he didn't have the balls to jump the curb like I did. And with that my adrenaline pumped.

"Yeah, nigga, you ain't got that in ya!" I shouted, sitting up in the driver's seat. Both of my hands were on the steering wheel, one maneuvering the big truck around small corners and the other on the horn ready to press down whenever the need came for me to run a stop sign or a light.

I pulled up to the accident scene just seconds before the other chaser who had been racing me to it. I could see the jealousy all in this nigga's face. He had to be sick. First of all, I beat him to the hit. Second, it was only one car. Apparently the driver lost control and ran into a light pole.

I jumped out the truck, clipboard in hand, and walked over to the passengers who were standing on the pavement looking in disbelief at their crashed newer-model BMW X5. I did a quick assessment of the vehicle as I walked past it to get to the owner. It looked to me like a home run. I was wide awake then.

I approached an older woman. She was just ending a call on her cell. Beside her stood a young bull, probably like thirteen, fourteen. He had to be her son. I thought about what I would say first to break the ice between the lady and me. I had to be sensitive to the fact that she had just been in an accident and was most likely fragile. Not to mention the fact that she was a white woman in a black neighborhood. And her posh demeanor gave me the impression that she was the type of white lady who would clutch her purse in the presence of a black man. Now here she was, forced to be out on the corner surrounded by a bunch of black people, bystanders and tow truck drivers alike. I didn't necessarily take her as being prejudiced, just sheltered and misinformed.

"Are you two all right?" I asked.

The woman shook her head yes, but her eyes told me that she wasn't. She looked like she was scared and shaken up all at once. Her son looked a little timid, too. He probably wasn't used to being around black people, either. *I gotta help make these people feel comfortable,* I thought. The first thing I learned about how to put at ease people who were in distress, and in this case fearful, as well, was to say something that would make them feel safe right away.

"The police are on their way," I said. And before the woman could ask me how I knew, I explained to her that I had a close relationship with the Eighteenth District and that I was the person they contracted with to handle accidents in the area. I handed her a business card with all the shop's information on it and explained that my father's body shop was close by. I told her I would gladly tow her car for her and securely lock it indoors at my dad's shop at no charge to her. Then I would help her set up an insurance claim, get her in a rental car, and have her adjuster come out to the shop to give us an estimate right away. That way my guys could get started repairing her car ASAP. She was feeling what I was saying and was even more compelled when I told her I could save her from having to pay the deductible.

By the time the cops arrived, there were about a half-dozen other chasers on the scene. They were green with envy, too. It had been slow for a while, at least for the past three weeks I had been back on the streets after training Leah. And it seemed whenever it did pick up and start hittin', it was only totals and junk. This was the first homer that any of us came across in a minute, and niggas was mad that it was me and not them who got it. I even noticed one chaser try to approach the lady after it was clear that I had been talking to her first. I wanted to knock the pussy out to show him not to disrespect me like that again. But I wasn't about to let him make me lose the job. So I kept my composure and, as politely as I could, told him to back the fuck up. He complied. One thing about the streets: my name rang bells in them. Between the work my pop put in before he opened the shop and the numerous niggas I done knocked out, niggas knew not to take shit too far.

The cops got out of their car, and I realized I knew them from being on accident scenes with them in the past. I greeted them with handshakes as they walked up to where the lady and I were standing. And it was that small gesture that sealed the deal for me. After giving her statement to the police, the lady agreed to let me tow her car. She signed the tow agreement I had written up, and then she got in the back of the ambulance to be taken to the hospital. Meanwhile, I hooked her car and towed it to the shop.

As I was pulling up in front of the shop, I noticed Leah was just opening up. My dad had given her the key two days ago as a one-month promotion-type thing. I threw my truck in park and jumped out to tease her.

"It's ya second day opening and you late? That's why you can't give a black person a promotion."

"Shut up," Leah said dryly, not even giving me the giggle that I usually got out of her.

"Is today not a good day?" I asked, unhooking the car.

"No, not really," she said, walking into the shop.

I followed behind her, determining I would bring the car I just towed inside later.

"What's wrong?"

"Nothing."

"You sure?"

"Yeah, I'm sure." She sighed.

"All right." I sighed back. "I ain't goin' hound you. I know you got some stuff to do before it get busy around here. But if you wanna talk about it, I'll be available at lunchtime at the Breakfast House on Fifty-Fourth and Woodland."

Leah managed to smirk. "Thank you," she said.

"No problem." Then I let her get to work as I drove the smashed-up BMW inside the shop. I left the tow agreement and the keys on Leah's desk so she could set up a file, and I rolled out, headed back to post up and listen to the scanners.

It was close to one o'clock when I walked into the Breakfast House. My stomach was growling and I could taste the fish and grits I planned on ordering. I took my coat off and sat down when I was alerted that I had a text message.

Does that lunch offer still stand? Leah

I wrote back, *I'm waitin' on you.* Then before I pressed Send, I wrote, *How you get my number?*

It was on the tow agreement, duh was her reply.

I laughed to myself as I imagined Leah saying all that with her usual sass. For the hell of it I wrote back *Oh, all right*, then put my phone back on my hip.

Although I knew what I wanted, I looked at the menu to pass time. I was hungry as hell, but I wasn't going to order until Leah got there. As soon as she walked in the door, though, I got the waitress's attention. Leah and I put in our orders and drank down our iced teas with peaches while we waited for our food.

"Let me ask you something," she broke the silence.

"What's that?" I asked, taking the opportunity to look into her light brown eyes.

"Why you always so nice to me?"

I chuckled and asked, "What you mean? I'm nice to everybody, ain't I?"

"Yeah, but you be extra nice to me. Even before I started working at the shop. Whenever Kenny brought you around, you would give me these looks . . . like you cared about me or something."

I could feel myself blush as I thought about how to explain myself to Leah. I mean, I was flattered to know that she noticed me lookin' at her. That meant she was lookin' back. And if she didn't bring it to Kenny's attention, that meant she liked it.

"Oh my God, look at you blushing." She caught me.

I chuckled again.

"What is it with you, Nasir? Matter of fact, I don't even wanna know. Just do me a favor. Spend some time with Kenny, and maybe whatever it is you feel for me will rub off on his sorry ass."

I nodded slowly. "So that's what's bothering you. You havin' man problems."

"I wish that was it," she said, putting her hand up on her forehead, then running her fingers through the front of her hair.

"What more is it?" I asked her. "That case y'all caught?"

"Humph, do you know he put that on me?" she revealed.

I frowned and asked, "What you mean?"

"Kenny wanted me to take that case by myself," she explained.

"For real? That's fucked up."

"No, what's fucked up is I would do something like that for him and he would still mess around on me."

I shook my head, and as I noticed Leah's eyes watering, I reached across the table and rubbed her shoulder. It was then that she broke down.

"Why you stay with 'im?" I mustered the nerve to ask.

"It used to be for the security," she said, wiping her tears with a napkin. "But now, I did something that kinda tied my hands to 'im."

"Hmm, you sound like me."

"What are you sayin'?" she probed.

"I did something while I was workin' with that nigga back when we used to chase together, and for him not sayin' nothin' I felt like I owed him. And he took full advantage of that shit, too . . ."

"That's Kenny for you."

"That's how he ended up with you," I mumbled.

"Huh?"

I looked up at Leah and decided to tell her the truth. "That's why I'm extra nice to you and be givin' you those looks," I said. "I feel bad that I let him get you."

"What do you mean, you 'let him get me'?"

"I saw you first. Matter of fact, I used to look forward to seeing you at ya bus stop. Every morning I made sure I was posted up at the same time to see you get on the Fifty-two. And then one day I was finally goin' say something to you, and this nigga come out of no-where talkin' about let him have you. I argued this nigga down, like, naw nigga, you wasn't thinkin' 'bout her 'til I said I was goin' try to talk to 'er. But he wouldn't let up. And him being Kenny, he dangled that shit I did over my head." I began to impersonate Kenny's voice and repeated what he had said to me some few years back. "Nigga, you owe me. If it wasn't for me, you would be locked up right now, not able to get at no pussy. So you can pass it up this one time."

"Oh, I was just a piece of pussy to y'all?" Leah questioned with a bit of attitude.

"Not to me. That was what that nigga said."

"So what did you say after that?"

"I was like, fuck it. You got it."

"So you gave me up that easy, huh?"

I shrugged my shoulders and said, "I ain't want to. Believe me, I didn't. But I felt like I ain't have no choice. You know what I mean?"

"I know exactly what you mean," Leah said with a more serious face. Then she put on her gorgeous smile and said, "Wow. That's deep. I ain't been on a bus since I dropped out of Community, and that was like two and a half years ago. So you been holdin' on to feelings for me for a minute."

I exhaled and nodded. "Yup. The middle of '05."

"Are you serious?" Leah asked, her facial expression filled with wonder.

"I'm dead serious. I was hopin' you wouldn't talk to Kenny. But you did, and y'all wound up fuckin' with each other. I ain't goin' lie, I was hurt. To this day, I wonder what it would have been like if you was my girl instead of his."

Almost immediately after I confessed to Leah about how I felt about her, it seemed a burden had been lifted off me. At the same time, though, I thought about my girl, Tara, and I wondered if I had made the right decision by sharing with Leah how much I felt her. Was I opening a can of worms?

Leah shook her head in amazement. "Oh my God," she said. "That's crazy. I knew I felt something from you. I just never said anything because I didn't want to jump to conclusions. Why did you wait all these years to tell me?"

"To be honest with you, after that shit went down between Kenny and my pop and Kenny stopped coming around, I didn't think I would ever see you again. Then on the rare occasions that I did see you, Kenny was right there by ya side. Shit, I'm surprised he let you work so close to me now without him being around."

CHASER

"He got his reasons, trust me. Kenny don't do nothin' that don't benefit Kenny."

"Well, when is Leah goin' start doin' stuff that benefit Leah?"

She thought about it for a moment then replied, "I'm workin' on it."

I leaned forward and decided to take a chance. "How 'bout now?" I suggested, kissing Leah on her lips.

Right then the waitress came and placed our food in front of us. We put our conversation on hold as we ate. In fact, for the remainder of lunch we were silent, and I didn't know whether to take it as a good thing or a bad thing. I mean, I still felt a strong connection to Leah, and it seemed the feeling was mutual, but I wasn't sure if I came on too strong too fast. I didn't say anything because I didn't want to push it, so I paid the bill, walked Leah to her car, and figured I'd see her when I saw her.

Leah

I was in my bedroom getting my clothes out of my closet for work the next day, and I couldn't take my mind off Nasir. I was still shocked from earlier in the day when he told me he'd wanted me before I was with Kenny. Had I known that then, shit, I would have never talked to Kenny. But realistically, with or without Nasir in the equation, I don't know what made me talk to Kenny in the first place. I mean, unlike Nasir, who looked good *and* was a sweetheart, Kenny was just all right, a six on a scale of one to ten, to be precise, and he was an asshole. Silly me, I guess I was attracted to his bad-boy persona. But now that I was older, that bad-boy shit didn't do anything for me but cause me heartache. I was so over it.

I was steam-ironing my shirt when I heard people come into the house. I turned the volume down on the sixty-inch plasma that hung on my bedroom wall, and I tuned into the mumbling that came from downstairs. It was Kenny and Dahwoo. I also could have sworn I heard the voice of a female but couldn't really make out who she was. Yet and still, what was any female doin' in my house? In the two years that I've been living with Kenny and in the year that we've been living in that house, Kenny has never brought a female to our place of residence. He brought guys there and only a select few, but never one female. He was very protective of where he laid his head, and he always used to say that girls ran their mouths too much for him to trust any of them with knowing where he lived. Not even his female relatives had been to any of our homes.

I stopped ironing, slid my feet into my Aspinal Nappa leather and suede slippers and went downstairs.

"What's up, Leah?" Dahwoo spoke to me as I got to the bottom of the steps.

"Hey, Woo," I replied, stopping to hug him on my way to the kitchen.

"What's up witchu, cuz?"

"Same ol', same ol'," I responded. Over Dahwoo's shoulder I looked down at Kenny's side chick, who they all thought I believed was Dahwoo's girl, sitting on my couch in my family room. I rolled my eyes at her. Then she had the nerve to speak.

"Hi, Leah," she said with a smile on her face.

I completely ignored her and continued to the kitchen. Kenny was at the table counting money. Three new Sneaker Villa bags were on the floor leaning against the chair he was sitting in.

"What's up?" he said, not taking his eyes off his money.

"You tell me," I said. "I ain't know you was bringin' company home."

"Since when do I have to report to you that I'm bringin' people to my crib?"

"I don't know. Since when do you bring bitches to ya crib? This is a first."

"Yo watch ya mouth." Kenny got defensive.

I chuckled. "Oh, my bad. I shouldn't have called her a bitch. Tell me somethin', would you get defensive like that if somebody called me a bitch?"

"Where you gettin' at, Leah?" Kenny finally paused on counting his money and looked up at me.

I pulled out a chair and sat down opposite him. I looked him dead in his eyes and said, "I'm just tryna get a feel for who comes first to you, her or me?"

Pap! Kenny backslapped me across my face so fast and hard I didn't know what hit me. And usually that would have been enough to shut me up. But not that evening. That evening I wanted to let Kenny know that I knew he was messin' around on me and it wasn't the fuck cool! I had kept quiet way too long, and it was eatin' at me. I couldn't hold it in anymore, and although I knew I was putting things in motion for me to leave Kenny sooner rather than later, I wanted to get it off my chest to him that he wasn't foolin' anybody and that he had crossed the line by bringing his other girl to our home.

"I guess that's my answer, huh?"

Kenny ignored me, gathered his money, and got up from the table. He went to grab the Sneaker Villa bags, and I beat him to it.

"Where you think you goin'?" I asked him, anger in my tone.

"That's none of ya got damn business," he said, snatching the bags from me and almost tearing them. He turned to walk out of the kitchen, and I followed him.

"What you tryna tell me, Kenny? Huh? What you tryna tell me by bringin' this bitch around me all the time? You tryna move her in on me? Huh? Let's be real!"

"Shut the fuck up!" Kenny snapped as he approached the garage door.

By this time, Dahwoo and the bitch were a couple steps behind

Kenny. As I approached them, the bitch said, "You hype for nothin', Leah. It's nothin' between Kenny and me."

"Bitch, I don't remember sayin' shit to you!" I yelled right before I lost control. I reached out and swung on the girl, and the next thing I knew we were fighting in my garage.

No sooner than we started did Kenny break it up. He grabbed me from behind, his arms wrapped around me like he was performing the Heimlich maneuver.

My pumping adrenaline started to decelerate as Kenny contained me. I felt like I was coming down off a high. And although it was just a short period of time that I was fist to cuffs with the broad, the fight actually had me feeling good. I was able to blow off some steam, which I hadn't been in a position to do in such a long time. And damn if I didn't need it.

And maybe it was a scene Kenny needed to see as well. Maybe he needed to see that side of me. He had gotten so used to my being passive, letting a lot of his ill behavior slide. Maybe seeing how upset I was over his disrespecting me would make him think twice about his actions. And at that point that was all it was about to me—the respect. Because it damn sure wasn't about our love life. That was over and done with as far as I was concerned. It was only a matter of time before Kenny would be getting locked up and I would be free from him. But until that day I was determined to get some respect out of his ass—some long-awaited and much-deserved respect.

Tossing Dahwoo the bags and a pair of car keys, Kenny ordered him and the girl to get in Kenny's Impala, the less flashy of his cars and the one in which he made drug runs. Meanwhile, Kenny had turned me around to face him. He grabbed my upper arms and started shaking me.

"Chill the fuck out!" he yelled, his eyes bulging with fury. "If I wanna replace you, I can at any moment! Keep actin' the fuck up, and

I will!" At that he released me, shoving me and causing me to lose my balance and fall on the garage floor.

He joined Dahwoo and the girl in his car. They backed out of the garage and pulled off. Boiling with anger, I jumped up off the floor and went inside my house, slamming the garage door behind me. *So much for demanding respect,* I thought. That nigga just took that bitch's side over mine and had me lookin' like an asshole. I got something for his ass!

I went upstairs, taking the steps two at a time, to my bedroom. I grabbed my cell phone off the dresser. Searching through my contacts for Dee-Dee, I pressed the Call button. While I waited for someone to pick up, I examined myself in the mirror. I was red-faced and I had some scratches on my nose and under my eye from the girl. But they were minor compared to the red scabby-looking sore in the corner of my mouth from Kenny.

"Hello," the detective answered on the second ring.

"Detective Daily," I said, trying to remain as calm as possible. "It's Leah Baker. Kenny just left our house with three kilos of cocaine. They're in Sneaker Villa shopping bags."

"Okay, good. Do you know where he's headed?"

"I'm not sure, but he was with the two people who got locked up with us that night. Dahwoo Courtland and the girl, whatever her name is. They're in a green Impala."

"Can you give me a license plate number on the vehicle?" the detective asked.

"I don't know it off hand. And they backed out of the garage, so it wasn't like I had the chance to see it. But I do know that he has to drop Dahwoo off at home, which is in the West Philly area."

"Yes, I have his address on file. I'll look into it."

The detective thanked me and I hung up. Then I called Nasir.

"Hello?" Nasir sounded confused.

"Nasir."

"Yeah. What's up, Leah."

"I never did get to thank you for lunch today."

"You thanked me by comin'." He was sweet as usual.

"Yeah, well, how 'bout I thank you again by comin'," I said boldly, losing myself in thoughts of payin' Kenny back.

"Come again?" he said.

"Yeah," I brought my voice down to about a whisper. "That's right, I wanna come . . . again."

Nasir chuckled. "Who is this playin' with me, man?"

"I'm not playin'," I told him, tears beginning to return. "Come get me, please."

"Leah, you serious?"

"Yes, Nasir."

"What about Kenny?"

"What about 'im?"

"All right." Nasir gave in. "I'm on my way."

Soon as I hung up the phone, I went in my bathroom and freshened up. I reapplied makeup, did my hair, and tried as best I could to cover the bruise Kenny had left on my lip. I changed into a pair of clean panties and a bra, and not just a Victoria's Secret set, either. I opted for one of my sets by Vagin Pouvoir. I put on a gray hologram Alexander McQueen sweater dress for easy access and a pair of black Alexander McQueen button-trim boots, threw on a black Doma waist-length leather jacket, grabbed my metallic Pauric Sweeney python pocketbook and my keys, and waited by the door.

I heard Nasir's truck as it drove down my street. There was no mistaking that loud Viper engine. I looked out the window with anticipation. Indeed, it was him. I opened my door and stepped out. It was dark and cold outside, so no one was out to see me creeping. Besides, my house was far enough away from both my neighbors and pretty obscured by the tall trees Kenny had had the landscapers plant for privacy; even if anyone was out, the chances of their seeing me were slim.

I took quick-paced baby steps to Nasir's truck, where he had parked along the curb.

"What's up?" Nasir greeted me as I got in the passenger seat.

"Hey." I blushed.

Suddenly I became nervous—like I was a fan around her favorite rapper. It was as if Nasir had put a spell on me. I mean, I was never so coy around him before, although I'd always found him attractive. I guessed it was because now I knew that he liked me, and when I thought about it, deep down inside I liked him, too. And true, indeed, it was a possibility that my feelings were amplified after having gone through that bullshit with Kenny. I had been pushed to the edge and practically into Nasir's arms. I was vulnerable, that I knew. But whatever the cause, I was feeling really giddy in Nasir's presence. I needed to pull myself together.

I tried to distract myself. I pulled the mirror down and began to fix my hair. One by one, I put the strands that got displaced by the light wind back in their rightful position. I could feel Nasir peek over at me a few times while I did so. I dug in my pocketbook and retrieved my lip gloss. I continued to look in the mirror as I applied a coat on my already glistening lips.

"You look good." Nasir broke the silence. "Even better than I imagined when you was teasin' me on the phone."

"Thank you," I said, not taking my eyes off myself.

"I wanna know to what I owe the occasion? I mean, don't get me wrong, I'm not complainin'. I'm not complainin' at all. You was talkin' to me dirty on the phone, then you come out here in ya little freak 'im dress lookin' all good. I'm just feelin' lucky as hell right now, and I wanna make sure what I'm feelin' is right."

I smirked but I didn't give Nasir a response, partly because I didn't have a response to give him and partly because I was still feeling shy.

CHASER

"What's wrong? Why are you so quiet now?"

Finally I closed the mirror and turned my attention to Nasir. I shook my head as if to say nothing.

"Something's wrong," he insisted. "Now tell me what's up. What's on your mind?" he asked.

I smiled and looked over at him, and it was the first time I really noticed his features. He had these big brown eyes that were mesmerizing and these thick, dark eyebrows that made him look mad even when he wasn't. And just the way he looked at me turned me on. I didn't know how to compose myself. He was dripping in sex appeal, and he had so much damn swagger. Between me wanting desperately to get revenge on Kenny and being in the presence of such a good-looking man who had deep feelings for me, I was open.

"What's up?" he asked, batting his eyes in a seductive manner to match the soft sexy tone of his voice.

"I don't know what has come over me, and I'm not usually this type of girl. But something about you, something about tonight, something about right now got me feelin' like I wanna do it to you so bad," I finally said to him, exuding somewhat of the same confidence I had on the phone.

Without saying a word, he leaned over, took his free hand, and firmly placed it on the back of my head. Then he started kissing me with the passion of Christ. And I damn sure felt like I was being saved. His lips were so succulent, his tongue gentle and alluring. Nothing like Kenny's rushed and uncalculating kisses. Instead, and much to my preference, with Nasir it seemed like he was trying to make me have an orgasm just by kissing me.

Nasir drove the truck through the neighborhood to an area where there were no houses, pulled over, put the truck in park, and turned off the headlights. All the while I was rubbing my fingers through his silky hair, and he caressed my breasts with one hand. It was at that moment that I realized Nasir and I might end up having sex right there in his truck, just minutes away from my home. And before I could overanalyze the situation and talk myself out of going through with fulfilling my desires, I forced myself to stop thinking about it. For once I was going to put my feelings before Kenny's. I was going to do what he had done to me on numerous occasions. I was going to cheat on him without regard to the possibility of his finding out. I was going to give him a dose of his own medicine and just go with the flow.

Once we were stationary, I unbuttoned Nasir's pants. Meanwhile, his hands were up my dress, working my panties down off my hips. His touch gave me goose bumps, and I was very much into it. The next thing I knew, my cell phone chimed. I glanced at it and saw that it was a text message. Lo and behold, it was from Kenny. My mental state changed in an instant. As if someone snapped me out of a trance, I went from being carefree and unscrupulous to being worried and mindful of my actions. *What am I doing,* I thought. *This isn't me.*

I paused the touchy-feely session with Nasir and read Kenny's text message. It said that he was on his way back to the house and to meet him at the door in twenty minutes with his house keys. He said he must have left them on the kitchen table.

"Oh my God," I mumbled, replying to the text.

"What's wrong?" Nasir asked, leaning in to kiss me on my neck and continue what we had started.

"I gotta get back home," I said as I texted Kenny.

Where are you? I wrote.

"What time?" Nasir asked, rubbing my thighs, unwilling to give in so easily.

"Now. Kenny is on his way back to the house, and he wants me to bring his keys to the front door," I said.

"Tell me you jokin'," Nasir said.

Then Kenny's reply came through. *I'm on Upland Way, leaving Woo house. I'll be there in 15 min.*

Before I wrote back, I held my cell phone up in front of Nasir's face so that he could read Kenny's text to me.

"You gotta take me home," I reiterated.

"Damn!" Nasir griped as he buttoned his pants back up. Then he put the car in drive and hauled ass to my house as if he was chasing a wreck.

Well, I'm in the tub, so drive kind of slow to give me time to get out, dry off, and meet you at the door. I wrote back, trying to slow Kenny down.

I started to straighten my clothes, but there was no need to. I would have to take them off as soon as I got in the house anyway. If Kenny were to see me with a whole new outfit on, he would know something was up. And he was the type who wouldn't address it right away, so you would never know if you were caught and therefore you wouldn't be able to make up a believable excuse. No, he'd rather make people pay for their wrongs without even letting them know that he knew they'd done something wrong.

U got bubbles in there?

Yes, I wrote, wondering what the hell he asked that for.

Bubble bath, huh? Well, now I'm goin' speed home so I can get in there with u.

Okay, I wrote. But I thought, *Hell no!*

"Nasir, please hurry," I said. "He is drawin', talkin' about he's speedin' home." I told Nasir only what I wanted him to know. The bubble-bath conversation would have been TMI. I didn't want him to go home with it on his mind that I was fucking Kenny after he had been the one to turn me on. It was bad enough that he didn't get to release like I was sure he had every intention on doing. I didn't want to add insult to injury.

"You think he know somethin'?" Nasir asked.

"I hope not."

When we got close to my house, I noticed a car turn down my

street ahead of us. It was dark, so I couldn't see what kind of car it was, but to be safe I had Nasir drive past my block, make a U-turn, and come back to see if the car had pulled up in my driveway or if it had kept going down my street. It was gone. Thank God.

Nasir pulled up in front of my neighbor's house. I had him drop me off there so if Kenny pulled up it wouldn't appear like there was someone at our house. After we said quick good-byes, I got out of Nasir's truck. I jogged past my neighbor's home and power walked through my lawn. Once in my front door, I ran upstairs and immediately ran bathwater. I took off all my clothes and put them away. I laid some pajamas out on my bed and turned on my TV to make it look like I was settled at home the whole time, as opposed to looking like I had just run in the house and jumped in the tub.

I went into the master bathroom and, before stepping into the Jacuzzi tub, looked under my sink for bubble bath. There was none, and it dawned on me that I had used the last of it two nights prior.

I heard the alarm system chirp that the garage door had opened. Shit! I nixed the bubble bath and got in the tub, turning the water off simultaneously. I laid my head against the back of the tub and closed my eyes. I tried hard to relax and get rid of the tension I felt from having to face Kenny just minutes after I'd been about to have sex with his friend.

I heard Kenny's footsteps approaching. I braced myself for what was to come.

"Where the bubbles?" Kenny asked as soon as he walked in the bathroom.

I opened my eyes slowly, as if they had been closed for a while. I looked in the tub and said, "Oh, they must've dissolved."

Kenny started undressing, leaving his clothes right where he stood, in the middle of the bathroom floor.

"Where's ya phone at?" Kenny asked, taking his cell phone out of its case on his belt. He placed the phone on the edge of the tub. "What, you got out the tub to text me?"

Shit. I thought I had covered all bases, but I forgot to bring my cell phone into the bathroom with me.

"It was getting wet when I was texting you back and forth, so I put it in the room. I ain't want it to get water damage," I said, thinking quickly.

I closed my eyes again as Kenny joined me in the tub, his body touching mine. Unlike Nasir's, Kenny's touch made me cringe. Whenever he would rub his leg against mine or touch me, I would move. I completely ignored him.

"I know you mad at me," he said, climbing on top of me. "I'm sorry."

I tried to maneuver from underneath him, but he wouldn't let me. Instead, he maintained his position between my legs.

Kissing me on my lips, he said, "Let's have make-up sex."

Ugh, I was disgusted. I didn't want to have sex with Kenny, especially not when I was still upset with him. But I didn't say anything. I just lay there, unresponsive. And as Kenny's lips roamed around on my neck and breasts and his penis found its way inside of me, I closed my eyes tight, imagining that it was Nasir and not Kenny who was in that tub with me.

Nasir

A week had gone by since I had told Leah the truth about how I felt about her and we had our moment in my truck. We had been sharing an attraction ever since. We kept our flirting to a minimum, though, not wanting anybody to know or even suspect that we had something going on. We didn't want word to get around to Kenny. Neither of us was ready for him to know that we had developed feelings for each other. Besides, as far as we were concerned, we were just testing the waters. It wasn't like we were trying to jump into a committed relationship with each other at that time. So a secret little fling was all it was, nothing deep enough to stir up drama.

It was Valentine's Day, and on top of the thousand-dollar Christian Louboutin shoes I bought my girl, I planned to stop chasing early, at around one, and take her to the movies to see *Welcome Home,*

Roscoe Jenkins and then downtown to the Continental to eat. But here it was goin' on five o'clock and I was still out working. It had been hittin' out, meaning there had been a lot of accidents being called. So I kept calling my girl and pushing our plans back because I didn't want to miss out on a hit.

As for Leah, I didn't have any plans with her at all. I was sure she would be tied up with Kenny. I did get her something, though. Something simple, a two-hundred-dollar gift certificate to Millennium, the spa she mentioned that she loved. I put it in a card and dropped it in her pocketbook at the shop that morning. I didn't know if she had seen it yet, but I assumed not since I hadn't gotten a thank-you phone call or a text.

I was sitting in the truck posted up at my spot in the gas station lot on Fifty-second and Spruce listening to the scanners. Whenever I was out working that was where you could find me, unless I had run to a hit or gone to the shop to either take a car or collect my commission.

Usually I would be in the truck by myself, but that time I was with my homie Brock and a young bull about nineteen, named Hype, who was another chaser who brought wrecks to my pop's shop.

Brock recently became interested in chasing, and so when it wasn't busy at the shop, he would get in the truck with me and learn the game. Hype, on the other hand, had his own truck he chased out of, but he had parked it and got inside mine to play me in a game of Madden on the PlayStation that I had installed in my truck. Hype sat in the passenger seat, his hands gripping the joystick and eyes glued to the animated football game that was displayed on the ten-inch TV screen. It was serious for us, too, because we bet money on our teams. Brock even bet money on the different plays.

The three of us were into the game, focused, until Brock squealed, "Aww, shit, look at the mothafuckin' wheels," a line from the movie *Menace to Society.*

Hype and I both broke our concentration and looked up. Driving up on the gas station parking lot and heading in our direction was a bad-ass yellow Lamborghini Gallardo coupe. I sat up to get a better look at the vehicle as it stopped right next to my truck on the passenger's side.

"Oh shit, that's ya bull Kenny drivin' that mafucka," Brock said when he got a glimpse of who was behind the wheel.

Just then Kenny hopped out the sports car and walked over to my truck. I rolled down my window as he approached my side.

"What's up, Nas," he greeted me with a handshake.

"Slow motion," I said. "I see you got a new wheel."

"Yeah, man, that's what I need to talk to you about," Kenny said.

What now, I thought. *What does this nigga want?* I got out of my truck.

"What's up?"

"Yo, Leah mad as shit at me, dog. She been walkin' around the house givin' me the silent treatment all week."

"Why? What you do?" I pretended I didn't know.

"I brought this joon to the crib. I tried to tell her it was my cousin's girl, but she ain't stupid. She wasn't goin' for that shit."

"All man, that's crazy."

Kenny scratched his head. "I know. I was wrong. But I'm tryna make it up. So I bought her that car and I wanna surprise her for Valentine's Day."

A quick feeling of jealousy shot through me as I calculated how my minute Valentine's Day gift to Leah could stand up against a fuckin' Lamborghini.

"Oh, all right," I said, unenthused. "That's hot."

"So I need you to help me set it up," he said.

Before I could say something, I was interrupted by the sound of my truck door opening.

It was Hype. He had my phone in his hand extending it out to me. "You missed a call from somebody named Le—"

Before he could reveal in front of Kenny that Leah had called me, I cut him off. "Oh, the Chinese bull whose car I towed yesterday," I said, making up something quickly. I took my phone, pressed the End button to clear the screen, and put it in the case on my hip. Hype gave me a suspicious look as he got back in my truck. I brushed him off and got back to Kenny, hoping he didn't peep it.

"What was you sayin'?" I asked.

Kenny smirked and said, "I was sayin' I need you to help me set up the surprise. I want you to somehow get Leah's keys and move her car out of her parking spot. Drive it around the corner or some shit. Then I'm goin' put the Lambo in her space with a big red bow around it."

"Oh yeah?"

"Yeah, that's crazy, ain't it," Kenny bragged.

"Yeah, that's bananas," I said. "So when you tryna do this?"

"Like now, 'cause I wanna catch her before she get off."

"Damn, man, you know five o'clock is rush hour. I don't be leavin' my post during rush hour."

Kenny put his hands up and gave me a look. "Dog, for me. Just this one time."

"All right, nigga," I huffed.

I got in my truck. Kenny got in the Lamborghini. He followed me to the shop. And the whole ride there I had to hear Brock's mouth about how Leah's panties were goin' melt off when she seen that Kenny had bought her a Lamborghini. I couldn't be mad at him, though, because of course he didn't know what Leah and me had goin' on. Like I mentioned earlier, nobody knew about Leah and me, and I wanted it to stay that way. But I wanted so bad to tell that nigga to shut the fuck up.

I walked in the shop holding my finger up to my lips to warn the workers not to say anything about the car that was outside. I knew once they saw it, there would be a bunch of loud-ass ooohs and ahhhs. I opened the door to the office, and Leah's face lit up with a smile.

"Heeey," she sang. "I just called you not too long ago. I wanted to thank you for my card and for treating me to the spa." She had a big smile across her face. "It's the best Valentine's Day gift ever." I didn't know if she was just stroking my ego or what, but I was sure Leah was used to getting grander gifts than that, and it was about to show.

"What's up," I said with way less energy than she gave me.

Her facial expression changed instantly.

"What's wrong with you?" she asked.

"Nothin'. I need the keys to ya car."

"Why, what's wrong?"

"I gotta move it real quick to get this car in the shop," I lied.

Leah reached down and opened the bottom drawer on her desk. She took her keys out and handed them to me. I took them and left the office. I didn't want to be long and give anybody reason to suspect anything.

I followed Kenny's instructions and parked Leah's car around the corner. I returned her keys and ran out of the shop like I had to hurry to an accident before she could start a conversation. Kenny did his part, and as the clock wound down we all waited outside the shop to see what Leah's reaction would be to her $200,000 Valentine's Day gift.

It was five after five when Leah came walking out of the shop. Kenny was kneeling down in the street between the Lamborghini and the car that was parked behind it. I was leaning against my truck, which I had double-parked in front of the shop. My dad, Brock, and a couple of workers were all standing near me.

"Surprise!" Kenny shouted as he popped up from behind the gift.

Leah screamed, "Oh my God! Kenny, what are you doin' here? And what is this? Where is my car?"

Handing her the keys to the Lamborghini, he said, "It's right here, baby."

Leah took the key and threw her hand over her mouth. She actually had tears in her eyes as she looked at all of us in amazement. I took a hard swallow watching her practically jump in Kenny's arms.

Then Brock didn't make things better when he nudged me and said, "Told you. Those panties is gone, dog!"

And on top of that even my dad was impressed. "That's a bad mothafucka right there," he said of the car. "I don't like the bull, but he did his thing with that. Shit, that car 'bout to make me cry out this bitch," he joked.

Leah got in the car and started looking at all its features. Kenny got in the passenger's side and assisted her. Then one of the workers yelled out, "Start it up. I wanna hear how it sound!"

Leah started the engine, and it roared. Then the same worker said, "Let me hear how it sound when you hit the gas!"

Leah put her foot on the gas pedal and drove out of the parking space. Niggas had goo-goo eyes watching her drive past us waving like she was Miss America. Not me, though. I was sick to my stomach, and I realized that no matter how close I got to Leah, she didn't belong to me. She was Kenny's, and despite the fact that she always complained to me about wanting to leave him, the truth of the matter was she wasn't goin' anywhere. I had to accept that. And I needed not to let her get in the way of what I had goin' on with my girl, whom I was with before Leah came into the picture. I still needed to keep my options open. It would had been stupid of me to put all my eggs in one basket, especially when that basket already had another nigga's eggs in it.

I called my girl. "Yo, babe," I said at the sound of Tara's voice.

"Don't 'yo, babe' me," she said, her attitude catching me off guard.

"Damn, what's wrong with you?"

"What's wrong with me? What's wrong with you? I took a half day at work today because you said you had plans for us, and then every hour on the hour I get a phone call pushing those plans back. Now here it is after five o'clock, and I still have yet to get time with you," she expressed. "I could've stayed at work for all this."

"I know. I'm sorry. It's just that it's been hittin' like crazy out here, and I been tryna get at this money."

"Is that really what it's been? Be truthful. Because I must admit I'm starting to think it's more you not making time for me anymore than chasing. I mean, you've been a workaholic since I met you, but you still made time for me. And lately, Nasir, that's been changing. It really seems like you are distancing yourself from me. And I have to say my instincts are tellin' me that you have someone else." Tara called me out on my recent change of behavior.

Damn, she hit the nail on the head, I thought. I didn't know what to say to her. I felt like lying to her would be no use, because she would know that I was doing just that. However, I didn't know how she would handle the truth, and if I told her, I would run the risk of losing her. And, of course, by my cheating with Leah, I was already running that risk, but I told myself that that could change. I could stop messin' around with Leah and keep the stable relationship I'd had with Tara before Leah came into the picture.

"So, what is it, Nasir? What's pulling you away from me?" Tara must have got tired of waiting for my response.

"It's not another girl, that's for sure," I said, deciding against telling Tara the truth. "But it is something," I added, wanting to give Tara some sort of justification for my behavior that would act as a diversion to her suspicions.

"What?" she asked.

"To be honest with you, I've been feeling under pressure about us gettin' a house together. It seem like every time we're together, that's all you talk about, and I don't know if I'm ready for all that now."

Tara exhaled, "Oh my God, boy. Is that it? That's what got you trippin'? Well, if that's the case, then hell, I won't bring up the house thing again until you're ready. I don't want to force you into anything, and I think our relationship is good as is."

"That was easy," I told Tara.

"It's always easy when you take time out to communicate," she said.

"Well, that's what I'm goin' do from now on. I'm goin' to communicate. And I'ma start by saying I'm sorry. I never meant to make you feel like I was distancing myself from you, and I damn sure never intended for you to feel like I had somebody else. I know that would hurt you, and that's the last thing I wanna do."

"Cool," Tara said simply.

"I'm on my way to get you so we can spend this evening the right way."

"I'm looking forward to it," she said.

"All right. I'll see you in a minute."

"Okay."

" 'Bye."

" 'Bye."

Driving from the shop to Tara's apartment at the Executive House on City Avenue, I did a lot of thinking, and I started to feel bad. Tara was a good girl, and I was messin' up on her. She didn't deserve what I was doing. I thought about how miserable Kenny's cheating made Leah, and I realized I was no better than that nigga. I told myself that I would stop dealing with Leah on a romantic level. We could remain friends, but that had to be it. I planned to reinvest my time and energy into somebody who was exclusive with me rather than gettin' caught up in Leah's hype. And despite the voice I heard in the back of my head telling me that it was going to be impossible for me to detach myself from Leah, I was determined to do that. But goddamn it. How? I wondered. Leah was magnetic. I was drawn to her and had been before I even met Tara. I was fighting with myself about what to do. But at the end of the day I knew it would come down to love verses lust. Reality verses fantasy. Which one would win, I had yet to find out.

Leah

It had been a long weekend for me, being that Kenny wanted me to take off Friday and enjoy my new car with him, and Monday was Presidents' Day. And in that time period Kenny spent a lot of time schooling me to his plan of how I could wash his money through the shop. I knew I'd have to deal with his scheme sooner or later. I didn't want to do it, of course, because I didn't want to jeopardize my good standings with Nasir or Vic, but I had to. It was the only way I'd be able to stay out of prison. So I figured I would try hard to remain undetected, and meanwhile stay on top of Kenny's dealings with hopes that I'd collect enough information so that Detective Daily would finally be able to get him on something substantial enough to arrest him. And everything that I was doing—from provoking arguments with Kenny to getting him to tell me things that he wouldn't usually tell me, from sitting in on meetings that I usually missed to working at the shop pretending to spy on Vic and Nasir—would be over.

So on Tuesday I arrived at work ready to put Kenny's plans into action. Out of the half-dozen people who worked at the shop, I had all but one on my list to incorporate in the scheme. The one person I excluded was the janitor, Brock. And it wasn't that I didn't like Brock that I decided not to include him. It was just that I knew his loyalty lay with Nasir. They were too close. Plus, Brock was the type of guy who liked to run his mouth. We were cool, yes, but he just wasn't a good candidate for what I was setting up. I had to address only those workers who I not only had a rapport with but who I felt I could trust not to say anything to anybody, especially Nasir.

I approached each one of them the minute he came in. And if two happened to come in together, I asked to speak to them one at a time. The first to arrive was the painter, Joe. He peeped his head in the office to say good morning like he did every day and to give me a copy of the *Metro*, a free newspaper that he normally picked up on the train. I liked reading my horoscope and doing the brain teasers and puzzles.

After handing me the paper, Joe started to disappear to the back of the shop, where he tended to cars in the paint booth all day. But before he got too far, I stopped him.

"Hey, Joe," I called out to him. "You got a minute?"

Joe stopped walking and turned around. He peeped his head back in the office.

"Yeah, what's up?" he asked.

I walked out of the office to talk to Joe on the floor, out of view of the cameras that were installed throughout the shop.

"I have a proposal for you," I said.

"Oh yeah, like what?"

"It involves you making an extra three hundred dollars per week on top of ya pay. And," I said, before he could start asking questions, "you would start getting your salary in cash instead of checks, so you don't have to worry about givin' a check-cashing place a percentage."

Joe nodded eagerly. "That sounds like a hell of a proposal. But what I gotta do to get it?"

"All you have to do is continue to do your job like you been doing and don't say anything to anybody about this deal."

"That sound too good to be true. What are you gettin' out the deal?"

"Your checks."

"My checks?"

"Yeah. Every Friday Vic gives you a check, right?"

"Yeah."

"Well, from now on, instead of you cashin' the check, you'll give it to me and I'll give you your earnings plus three hundred."

"And what you goin' do with my checks?"

"Now, if I tell you that, then I will feel like I can't trust you anymore and won't be able to do the deal with you. I will say this, though: it's not gonna hurt anybody, and it's not gonna cause nobody to lose any money—that's if and only if you do not tell anybody. Absolutely nobody." I emphasized the importance of keeping the deal silent.

Joe sighed and looked around the shop, as if he were giving what I said some thought. I knew he wanted to say yes—I was offering him something hard to refuse—but I understood his caution. I decided to throw in an incentive to get a quick yes before all his pondering led to a no and possibly even to a talk with Vic.

"How 'bout I give you a five-hundred-dollar sign-on bonus right now?"

"Aww, man, you for real, huh?"

"I wouldn't play with you about something like this. Now I know times are hard and you could use the extra money," I said, taking five one-hundred-dollar bills from my pants pocket and placing them in Joe's hand.

CHASER

He looked down at the bills and, with a smirk on his face, slid them in his pocket.

"I take that as a yes," I said.

Joe nodded. "I don't have to do nothin', right?"

"Nothin' more than what I said."

"All right," Joe said. "It's a yes."

Throughout the morning, I had that same conversation with the other four of Vic's employees who were on my list, and they all ended the same way. Well, not exactly the same. The frame guy, Porter, was skeptical about the fact that he had to keep our deal a secret. He asked if there was nothing wrong with what I was proposing, why did I insist he not tell anybody. I used reverse psychology on him, a trick my mom used to use on my sister and me all the time when we were kids.

"Do you think you have a drinking problem, Porter?" I asked him.

His eyes grew big, and rather defensively he answered, "No!"

"Do you think there's anything wrong with you taking a drink here and there while you're on the job?"

"I mean, it's just to take the edge off sometimes, you know. But it doesn't affect my work or anything, so I don't see it as a problem, no."

"Well, why don't you tell Vic that sometimes, just to take the edge off, you go out back or into the bathroom and take a swig of vodka while you're on the clock?"

"I got your point," Porter said. "Some things that we feel aren't a problem may not fly with the boss, and so it's better for everybody if we keep them to ourselves."

I nodded and smiled. Then I gave Porter his sign-on bonus. He agreed to the terms of our deal and happily went about his way.

The others had no problem with keeping their mouths shut. Shit, the economy was in a recession, so all they needed to hear was extra pay and they were with it. I even got the parts manager, Fred, to start giving me all the checks he would normally use to pay for parts in exchange for the cash. So basically, when parts would be delivered to the shop, instead of Fred giving the distributor a check for payment, he would give him cash, which would come from me, and then he would turn the check over to me. He would even leave the *Make payable to* line blank, saving me from having to doctor the check up later. And he agreed to do all that at no extra charge, which was good because that actually presented the opportunity for me to give myself the bonus I would have otherwise given Fred. And with that I would be able to build a stash of my own without Kenny knowing.

Friday rolled around, and everybody stuck to the plan, secretly handing over to me their checks by placing them in magazines I had on my desk in exchange for the earnings plus an additional sum in cash, which I would leave in various hiding places in the bathroom. For example, Joe the painter knew to retrieve his money from inside the toilet tank cover, and Porter knew to get his from in the middle of the roll of toilet paper. Each one had a specific time to go into the bathroom and get his money, too. And I spaced the times out so it wouldn't be a nonstop flow of traffic going to the bathroom. I didn't want it to look suspicious.

I took the checks home to Kenny, who had some girls he knew wash the checks using nail polish remover to erase the names Vic had printed on them and rewrite them out to various phony LLCs that Sammy had helped Kenny form. Then I was responsible for depositing the checks in different business accounts that corresponded with the LLCs.

By that following Tuesday, the checks had all cleared, and Kenny had been able to clean up thousands of dollars in just four days. And because we weren't increasing the amount payable, thus giving Vic any reason to look up the checks after they'd been cashed, we were able to get away with it, and Kenny's plan had worked. By the end of the first month Kenny cleaned up fifty-four thousand dollars. As for me, I was able to stash twelve thousand and while I felt bad for involving Nasir's dad in Kenny's money-laundering scheme, being able to make money of my own and create independence from Kenny was worth it to me. I only hoped Nasir would understand that, if ever a need came for me to explain myself.

In the meantime, Nasir and I maintained a complicated relationship. One minute he was pulling back, and the next he was all over me. I couldn't complain, though, because I figured it was hard for him to commit fully to me since I was with Kenny. So I played his game, following his lead. Whenever he acted like just a friend, I reciprocated; when he was in the mood to be more than that, I embraced that as well.

Overall, though, we kept our feelings for each other on the low, although at times it was difficult to contain ourselves when we were around each other. We had such an intense sexual attraction to each other that I would have thought people would notice just by the way we looked at each other. But so far no one seemed to be able to tell. And we took no chances in changing that dynamic. We expressed how we felt only when we were in private, which was usually during lunch at the Breakfast House.

We had become regulars at the quaint diner-style restaurant and very familiar with its restrooms, where Nasir and I managed to release our charged sexual energy on several occasions. And like I had imagined, sex with Nasir was pleasurable beyond belief. Between my being extremely attracted to him and his having an impressive-sized part, I found myself in a state of heavenly bliss every time we did it. It didn't even matter that it normally lasted only five minutes and consisted of our standing in not-so-comfortable positions, almost fully clothed, and burdened with nervous thoughts of being caught. In fact, all of the cons seemed to add to the adventure of our carrying on a forbidden love affair. And although there had been only a sexual relationship between Nasir and me up to that point, I must say, my feelings for him were growing beyond that. I was really starting to feel for the boy.

"I'm so glad winter is almost over," I said, sprinkling salt on my chicken fingers. "I cannot stand the cold. And when I get rich I'm movin' to Orlando, where it's hot all year round. I'm goin' open up a Disney-themed hair salon for kids. I'ma make it like a tourist attraction."

"Is that right?" Nasir asked, chewing his grilled-chicken sandwich.

"Yes, it is, and can you please chew your food before questioning my dreams. That's nasty."

He gave me the courtesy of finishing his bite before speaking again, then he said, "I'm not questioning your dreams. I'm makin' sure you serious, 'cause if you are, I'm goin' with you. I can't stand the cold, either."

"Who said you were invited?" I teased.

"Oh, that's right. That spot is already reserved for Kenny. My bad," he shot back, a little jealousy in his tone.

"Oh hell, no, it is not!" I snapped. "The day I leave Philly will be the day I leave Kenny."

"And that's not goin' be 'til you rich, huh?"

"Well, you know," I said, breaking a chicken finger in half and putting a piece in my mouth. "When I get enough money to stand on my own two."

"What if you had somebody like me to help you do that?" Nasir quizzed, looking me in my eyes.

"No, thank you," I shot his offer down. "I'm not tryna put myself in a position to depend solely on a man again. That shit's a trap."

Nasir nodded, "I respect that." Then he took another bite of his sandwich.

"Speaking of which, I'm surprised you don't have a girl you trick on. You are that type. The good looks, the nice-sized pockets, the street fame to a certain degree."

"Naw, I'm not that type at all. My money and my time are more valuable than that. If I'm goin' spend either one of them on a girl, it gotta be somebody I got plans for. And right now I haven't found that somebody yet."

I smiled and put another piece of chicken finger in my mouth.

"Naw, I'm just bullshittin'. I'm tryna make you that girl I trick on. What you think I got you here for?" Nasir joked.

I chuckled and playfully smacked his hand. "You so stupid," I said, although I believed that Nasir was serious about what he was proposing—that, deep down, he wanted me to be his girl. And even though I liked him a lot and wouldn't have minded being his girl, I wasn't ready for that yet. I didn't want to take Nasir's and my relationship any further, at least until I was able to cut my ties to Kenny. Until then it was best that Nasir and I continued at the pace we were going.

Nasir and I finished up lunch the way we normally did, talking about things other than a possible relationship between us. Instead, we caught each other up on current events, on what music videos we've seen lately and what reality shows we planned to watch that evening.

Afterward Nasir and I left the restaurant, and he walked me to my car, which was parked on the next block.

"Well, as always, I had a nice time," I told him, pressing the Unlock button on my keypad.

"Yeah, definitely," he said.

Then without warning, as I was opening my car door, Nasir reached out and put his arms around my neck, resting his elbows on my shoulders. His back against my car, he pulled me into him, placing my head on his chest. His head gently resting on mine, he whispered in my ear, "I'm not ready to leave you yet."

I raised my head and gave him a kiss on his lips. "Neither am I," I said.

"Let's go back in then," he suggested.

"And do what?" I asked.

"Have dessert," he said seductively.

I didn't say anything. Instead, I let my actions speak. I closed my car door back, relocked it, and followed Nasir back into the restaurant. He went in the restroom first, and a couple minutes later I went in behind him. It was a one-person bathroom, so we locked the door and got at each other instantly. We kissed while we removed our bottoms just enough to allow entry from Nasir's throbbing manhood into my yearning, most-prized possession. Seven minutes and about a hundred quick strokes later, Nasir climaxed and we were redressing. I didn't have an orgasm that day, but I was satisfied.

I left to go back to work and was feeling so refreshed. It was always a pleasure spending time with Nasir, and I meant that in every aspect of the word. I valued every second I got to spend with him and wished that our time alone could expand past an hour-long lunch break two or three times a week.

Nasir

Winter was officially over, and a change in the season meant a change in people. Not only was the sun out in full force, but so was the whole city. It seemed like everybody had come out of hibernation. Just thirty days ago you would have thought Philadelphia was a ghost town. I was kissing Leah in public without worry. But not anymore. The streets were flooded with people enjoying the warmer weather. *The difference a month made,* I thought.

"Why ain't nobody answerin' the phone?" I thought aloud as I hung up and redialed the shop. Still no answer. I didn't want to call Leah on her cell phone, but I had no choice, seeing as she wasn't answerin' the office phone.

"Hello," she answered, seemingly confused.

"Can you talk?"

"Yes."

"I didn't wanna call you on ya cell, but ain't nobody answerin' the office phone."

"Oh, everybody done left."

"It's only four o'clock. Y'all niggas got a hour left."

"It's the first day of spring. It's all nice outside. Niggas was itchin' to get off. And since ya dad was in a good mood after the guys finished a car, released it to the customer, and got the check, he told us we could leave early."

"Well, shit, I got a hit that I'm about to bring there and the customer wanna come to the shop and set up their claim and try to get in a rental today. Where you at?"

"I was on my way to get my car detailed."

"Can you do me a favor?"

"What, go back to the shop and help ya customer set up a claim?"

"Please."

"I would if I could, but after I told Kenny that I got off early, he made me an appointment at the detail shop. And if I miss that appointment and come home with a dirty car he goin' throw a fit."

"Man, tell that nigga somethin' came up. There's been a change of plans and you had to stay at work a little later."

Leah sighed, "All right. Let me call him and see what he say, then I'll call you back."

"All right. And, yo, tell 'im if you miss the appointment, you'll have one of the workers at the shop detail ya car for you."

"Okay, Nasir. Only for you," Leah said. "But listen, if I do have to wind up gettin' somebody at the shop to wash my car, can it be you?"

"Tomorrow?"

"No! Today, after ya customer leave!"

"During rush hour? You know that's the busiest time for a nigga in my line of work."

"Look, I'm givin' up my time for you."

"All right. All right. Whatever. Just meet me at the shop."

I hung up with Leah and hooked the crashed 2008 Pathfinder I had just got to my tow truck. The owner of the vehicle and I then got in my truck and headed to the shop. On our way there Leah called me back and told me it was cool and she could meet me, but that Kenny didn't seem too happy about it. She told me that I had gotten her in trouble and emphasized the fact that I owed her.

Once my customer and I got to the shop, Leah was sitting inside the office with a file out, ready to start the process of setting up a claim. While I unhooked the Pathfinder and found a place to store it in the shop, Leah got to work calling All State for the customer. It took about forty minutes for her to have all the paperwork filled out and signed, for the insurance company to issue a claim number and schedule a day for the adjuster to come out and look over the car, and to have an Enterprise rental-car representative come to the shop to pick up my customer and take her to get a rental.

Leah had come a long way since she first started working at the shop in January. I watched her work like a proud father. But was turned on like I was her man. At that, I knew it was time for me to go. It had been one of those weeks when I had been trying to keep my word to my girl, Tara, that I would be faithful to her. She had been comin' at me about distancin' myself again, and she swore me down that she knew I was messin' around on her. I denied all claims and smoothed things out with her. And again I told myself to chill on Leah. So after my customer left, I planned to leave right behind him.

"Good lookin' out, Leah," I said as I walked toward the door.

"Where you think you goin'?" she asked. "You gotta detail my car."

"I said only if you miss ya appointment."

"And I did miss it. It was for five o'clock. It's four fifty-six right now," she said, looking at her cell phone screen. "Ain't no way I'm goin' make it."

"All right, fuck it," I said. "Let me knock this out real quick."

I walked back toward Leah. I rolled up my sleeves and took my watch off, gently placing it on Leah's desk.

Leah reached for my watch and turned it over to look at the face. "What's this, a Bell and Ross?"

I smiled and said, "Look at you. You got a nice lil' eye."

She smiled back and said, "And you got a nice lil' collection of wrist wear. I be noticin'."

I chuckled at her comment, feelin' good that she paid that much attention to me and impressed at her knowledge of high-end watches. That quality made me like Leah that much more. Most girls didn't know anything past a Rolex.

She shot me a quick glance, then got up from her chair and headed out of the office and onto the floor.

I followed Leah over to her car, which was pulled up into the shop. She got inside to roll the windows up while I retrieved the water hose from the side of the shop.

I had every intention of washing Leah's car and getting back to work. But it didn't go down that way. Shortly after I turned on the hose and playfully wet Leah's shirt, my focus was rerouted. I guessed the cold water made her nipples hard, causing them to poke through her bra and her fitted white shirt. I was instantly turned on and started paying more attention to her breasts than to washing the car.

She noticed, of course, and flirtatiously asked, "You see somethin' you like?"

"I do, yeah," I said.

"Then put a down payment on it," she teased, walking up to me and brushing her body against mine.

I laughed and said, "Get outta here." I tried to refocus on washing the car. I truly didn't want to cheat on my girl that day. But there I was, in a position that I just couldn't resist.

Then, without thinking or saying anything more, we found ourselves in each other's arms, kissing and fondling. The sexual tension between us had always been so thick that whenever we had the opportunity to do so, relieving it became top priority.

"You tryna get us caught?" I asked, my way of giving myself one more out.

"By who? Ain't nobody comin' in here at this hour," she whispered as she ground against me vigorously.

"You right," I said, falling into her trap.

At that point I was so aroused I had no win in being faithful.

I turned the hose off and allowed Leah to have her way with me. She completely took charge, too. She opened her passenger's-side door and pushed me into the seat. She knelt down in front of me and unbuckled my belt, rubbing my dick simultaneously.

Meanwhile, I lifted her shirt up over her head and unsnapped her bra. I started haphazardly rubbing and playing with her nipples, all while trying to retrieve a condom from the wallet in my back pocket. I was fully erect as I opened the condom wrapper and started to put it on.

By that time Leah had pulled down her jeans and straddled my lap. She moved my hands out of the way and thrust me inside her. I almost exploded. She was so wet and so tight. It was so good, I started arguing with myself in my head. First about my girl: Why couldn't I have the same attraction and feelings for Tara that I had for Leah? If I could, it would have been easy to be faithful. Then I cursed myself out for lettin' Leah end up with Kenny in the first place. She was supposed to have been mine. All of her—her beauty, her wit, her intelligence, and, got damn, her pussy. I was feelin' some type of way, like I wanted Leah to stop fuckin' with Kenny altogether and just be my girl. And maybe she had me open, but I was ready to give up Tara for her and everything.

When we were done, we were both breathing like we'd run a marathon.

"Yo, roll the windows down," I said, out of breath. "It's hot as hell in here."

Leah climbed across to the driver's seat and turned the car on with her key, which was already in the ignition. Then she rolled down the windows.

Trying to have sex in the passenger seat of a car was hard enough, let alone a small-ass two-seater. We wounded up sitting in the car for a good fifteen minutes, just trying to get our strength back. While we were putting our clothes back on, we noticed the shop's overhead door started to roll up slowly.

"Who the fuck?" I blurted out, quickly trying to buckle my belt.

"Oh my God, oh my God," Leah panicked as she scrambled to put on her shirt.

I got out of the car and went to turn the hose back on so that whoever it was coming in the shop would believe us when we told them we were washing the car.

Just then my dad appeared from under the overhead door.

"What's up, Nas?" my dad asked as he walked over toward me.

"What's up, Dad?" I returned the greeting. I hosed down the front of Leah's car, avoiding eye contact with him.

My dad got close and noticed Leah in the driver's seat. She smiled and waved.

"Hi, Mr. Vic," she said.

"You just goin' sit in the car with the windows rolled down while he wash it?" my dad asked. I glanced up and could tell by his demeanor that he suspected something.

He walked around to the passenger's side and opened up the door. He pressed the button to roll up the window and then he paused for a second. He reached down in the seat and came back up. Holding the empty condom wrapper in his hand, he blurted, "Y'all was fuckin'?"

Leah and I didn't say anything. I lowered the hose, looked at my dad, and rubbed my goatee.

"Ain't you Kenny's girl?" my dad asked rhetorically.

Leah didn't say anything. She just looked at me like she wanted to ask me what she should do.

"Dad, it's not like that," I finally spoke up.

"Nas, you can say what you want. I know what it is."

Then Leah decided to speak up. "Mr. Vic, I am so sorry," was all she could offer.

My dad shook his head. "Don't be," he said as he backed away from the car and walked toward the office. "Nas, let me holla at you."

I turned the hose off and gave Leah a look like *Fuck* as I passed her.

"Leah, you might as well go 'head home," my dad called out.

Leah got out of the car and stood by the driver's side. "I'm so, so sorry, Mr. Vic," she offered once more. "You won't ever have to worry about this again."

"I know," my dad said. "Because you won't work here anymore."

"Dad," I said, trying to think of the right words that might influence him to give us a second chance.

"You're fired, Leah," my dad said plainly.

"Dad, seriously, we were just kissing and stuff, and we was about to but we didn't. And then you walked in. And if you let her keep her job, I give you my word I'll never do nothin' like this again," I pleaded.

"Mr. Vic," Leah whined. "I did not mean to disrespect your business. Please, Mr. Vic—"

"It's deeper than that, Leah. Now go 'head home before I call ya man and you have to explain this to him," said my dad coldheartedly.

Leah broke down in tears, gave me one last look of hopelessness, and then got in her car and drove it out of the shop.

"Dad, I know we wrong, but you ain't have to go so hard on her," I said.

"I did, Nasir. Because if I didn't, then I wouldn't be gettin' a message across! Do you know what kinda heat you bringin' to this shop and to our family by messin' around with that nigga's girl? If he find out you fuckin' his girl in my shop, he goin' want a mafuckin' war, Nas. And while I can afford one, I ain't tryna have one over no broad. Me and him already got bad blood. And I did you a favor by lettin' his girl work in this mafucka despite that. And you turn around and do some shit like this. What is you thinkin'?" my dad snapped. "And what the *fuck* you not out on the streets for? Huh? It's the middle of fuckin' rush hour! Man, go post up. I'll holla at you later."

I wanted to talk to my dad some more to try to smooth things over, but he wasn't goin' hear nothin' I had to say. So I did what I was told and went out on the streets to work. I left the shop mad as shit—at the situation, not at my dad. My dad had a valid point. I was drawin' by messin' with Leah behind Kenny's back. Despite how he got her, she was his girl. And despite the fact that we weren't close like we used to be, he was still my homie. I was in the wrong. I had to face that. And I told myself that I would have to leave Leah alone once and for all. I knew it was goin' to be hard, because I was feelin' the shit out the girl. But it was something I had to do. For real.

Leah

I was shook up driving home after Vic caught Nasir and me in the shop. How was I goin' to explain comin' home without the car washed? What was I goin' to tell Kenny was the reason for me gettin' fired? I couldn't make up no bullshit excuse, because that would fuck around and prompt Kenny to go to the shop ready to curse Vic out, and then Vic would tell Kenny what it really was. And that would be the death of me.

Just thinking about the mess I was in had me unable to stop crying. I decided to pull over in the Kentucky Fried Chicken parking lot on Forty-fourth and Market. I had to get my thoughts together and calm myself down. No way I was goin' home in the state I was in.

I leaned my head on the steering wheel and cried my last tears. Then I straightened up. I pulled the driver's-side mirror down and looked at my reflection, then I wiped my face and reapplied my makeup—mascara, eyeliner, and a fresh coat of lip gloss. All the while I was thinking about what I was going to tell Kenny.

Okay, I thought. *As far as the car, the guy couldn't wait around while I finished setting up the claim, so he promised he would wash it in the morning. Cool. But if I went with that, I wouldn't be able to tell him I got fired. Well, actually I couldn't tell him I got fired no matter what. I had absolutely no reason to give him that wouldn't prompt a bunch of questions and doubts. So hell, I'm not tellin' him I got fired.*

After about ten minutes of contemplating and coaching myself how I was to act once I got home, I was ready to face Kenny.

I drove out of the parking lot and made a left onto Market Street. I took it to Forty-sixth and made a right. I took Forty-sixth to Girard, then Girard to Belmont, Belmont across City Avenue, and I went home.

When I pulled in my driveway, I noticed that all three of Kenny's cars—the Maserati, the Suburban, and the Impala—were there. Kenny was, indeed, home.

I walked in the door. The TV was on in the family room, but no one was in there watching it. I turned it off. I went in the kitchen and dropped my pocketbook down on one of the bar stools. Then I got a glass out of the cabinet and put it under the ice then the water dispensers on the Viking side-by-side refrigerator. It was then that I heard Kenny's footsteps trotting down the steps. I braced myself.

"What's up," he said, upon landing in the kitchen.

"Hey," I said softly, sipping my ice water.

"You got the wheel washed?"

I shook my head.

Kenny's frowned. "Why not?"

"The claim I had to set up took longer than I expected, and the detailer couldn't wait. He said tomorrow morning he'll do it first thing," I conjured.

CHASER

Kenny didn't say anything. He just sized me up with his eyes.

"What?" I asked, breaking the creepy silence and trying to lighten the mood in the room.

Then Kenny blurted out, "I wanna fuck you."

My heart sank as I thought about what would happen if I had to pull my pants down right then and there and Kenny got whiff of the fact that I'd just had sex.

"I'm flattered, but I am so tired. It's been one of those days," I said. I put my glass in the dishwasher and went to go up the steps.

Kenny stopped me as I tried to walk past him. "Come here, man. I don't wanna hear that you-tired shit. Not today. I been waitin' for you to come home. You see I ain't out in the streets," he explained, pulling me by my arm closer to him.

"I knooow," I sang. "But really, Kenny. You don't understand. I am beat." I relieved myself of his hold and started toward the stairs again.

"You cheatin' on me with one of them niggas at the shop?" Kenny asked, stopping me in my tracks.

"No! Why would you ask me that?" I responded, neglecting to turn around and look at Kenny.

" 'Cause ever since you got that job you ain't been wantin' to fuck me no more," he complained. "And I know how it be at jobs. A ma-fucka like you, you like him, y'all start flirtin', and the next thing you know you stayin' at work late and y'all fuckin' on the desk while ain't nobody there," Kenny ran down his theory.

Kenny almost had it right. My desire to have sex had diminished. Not necessarily since working at the shop, but since he tried to give me that fraud case and spare his cousin and the bitch he was fuckin'. That was really what had made me lose interest.

"Kenny, no, I'm not cheatin' on you. You're right, our sex life hasn't been as active since I started workin', but that's only because I've been more tired now. Workin' takes your energy away," I reasoned.

Kenny was silent for a moment. Then he said, "I'ma ride with that answer for now. But go up there and lay down for a minute, 'cause I'm tryin' to get at you tonight, and I don't want to hear nothin'."

"Okay. Fine," I said, continuing up the steps.

Oh God, I thought as I got in my bedroom and plopped down on the bed. It may not have looked like it, but the mounting pressure of having to uphold so many lies and secrets was starting to wear on me. I didn't know how much more I could take, especially now that I had been fired and that was yet another secret I had to keep.

The next day I woke up early, as if I was going to work, but instead I made plans to go to the spa. I was mentally drained, physically exhausted, and emotionally torn. I needed a hot stone massage and milk bath so bad. I went to Millennium and used the gift certificate that I had gotten from Nasir. It made me think of him the whole time I was getting pampered. I wanted to see him.

After taking the day to relax at the spa, I showed up at the shop at a quarter after four to get my personal belongings and my paycheck. Everybody was cheerful as they were every Friday. Not only was it the start of the weekend, but it was payday as well. The minute I stepped foot in the office, Joe approached me.

Removing the mask from his face that protected him from inhaling fumes while inside the paint booth, he said, "You're late as hell today. I thought you wasn't comin' in. I thought I was goin' have to go to the check-cashing place after work."

"I wasn't gonna come in, but I had to get my stuff," I told him, putting my crossword-puzzle book into my bag.

"What you mean you had to come get your stuff? You leavin' us?"

"I got fired," I said honestly.

"Whyyy?" he asked, a concerned look on his face.

I smirked. "It had nothing to do with what we got goin' on. Don't worry. You're not next," I assured him. "It's a personal issue between Vic and me. But," I said, taking a few envelopes out of my pocketbook, "I still wanna keep our deal. In this envelope are instructions as to where and when to meet me every Friday. And can you give the others their envelopes as well? I don't wanna be seen giving shit to people on my way out the door. And tell them to take the instructions home and throw them in the trash. I don't need somebody stumbling across them here."

Joe nodded. "Yeah, sure," he said. "Damn, I hate to see you go, though. What happened?"

I shook my head. "It's a long story. And I really don't wanna tell it. Besides, you better get back to work before Vic walk up in here."

Joe looked at his wristwatch. "Yeah, he'll be walking in any minute now," he said. "Well, good luck. And I guess I'll see you next Friday."

I nodded and continued packing my things. Vic came in the shop at about four thirty-five. He made payroll, getting to me last. He didn't say anything to me. He just handed me my six-hundred-dollar paycheck and let me go about my business. I got in my car and drove around the corner to the 7-Eleven. I parked and waited in my car. At about five fifteen a few workers from the shop came pulling up into the parking lot. We exchanged checks and cash and then parted ways. My nerves were so jittery that I had to drive around awhile to calm them before driving to Nasir's post on Fifty-second and Spruce to see if he was out chasing.

I was waiting for the light to turn green when I noticed Nasir's truck speed out of the gas-station parking lot. I called him to let him know that I was pulling up so that he would slow down.

"Hey," I sang as soon as he answered his phone.

"What's up?" he said plainly.

"You don't sound happy to hear from me."

"Naw, I am. I'm just tryna get to this hit, that's all."

"Well, I'm behind you. I got a little bit of time on my hands, so I thought I'd get up with you."

"Oh word? Well, I'm about to go to this hit right now. What you doin' later?"

I called myself surprising Nasir, but it was him and his nonchalant attitude that surprised me. I didn't expect an answer like that. I thought he'd be happy as hell to spend a little bit of time with me, especially since our time together was limited. But, instead, it seemed he was brushing me off. I hoped he wasn't on some other shit since his dad had caught us yesterday.

"I'm not goin' be available later. That's why I'm here now," I said.

"Yeah, well, I'm goin' to a—"

"A hit, I know, I heard you. I can follow you, and then after you finish up we can go somewhere," I pressed.

Nasir was silent for a minute.

"What's the problem?" I probed.

"Nothin'. Let me call you right back." He hung up.

Something was goin' on with Nasir, and I was about to find out what that was. I continued following until I had the opportunity to pull up beside him. I rode alongside the curb and stopped at the red light beside his truck. Once aligned with him, I saw what the problem was: he had a girl in his passenger's seat. I beeped my horn.

The girl looked over at me. She had light brown skin, hazel eyes, and blond hair. She reminded me of Eva Pigford from *America's Next Top Model*, except she had a fuller face and was older-looking, and instead of a short cut her hair was pulled up into a loose ponytail. She was pretty.

The girl said something to Nasir, then he leaned up in his seat to look over at me. I shook my head at him and asked, "Is this a result of us being caught by ya dad yesterday? Or did you have this goin' on all along?"

Nasir had an angry look on his face, and he responded, "What? What are you talkin' about? You drawin' right now!"

At that point the girl had a question. "Who is that?"

"She work at my dad's shop. She's the secretary," he answered in a frustrated tone.

"He's right," I said with much attitude, "I'm just the secretary at his dad's shop."

"Leah, what is wrong with you, dog? You trippin'!" Nasir told me, clearly upset.

"I'm trippin'?" I quizzed. "You trippin'! Why you ain't just tell me you had somebody from the rip, and this wouldn't be goin' down right now!"

"Wait a minute, hold up," the girl butted in. "Why does she need to know that you have a girlfriend? What's really goin' on with y'all, Nasir? Is she the one that's been distractin' you lately?"

Nasir went to speak but the light turned green, and all the cars that were lined up behind us were blowing their horns all crazy so I couldn't hear him. All I knew was that right after he said whatever he said, the girl started swinging on him. He managed to pull off and drive up a block but rather erratically. And the next corner was as far as he got before having to pull over. I was right behind him, too. I wanted an explanation.

I was so mad. And don't get me wrong, I was not mad that Nasir had a girl with him. No! What pissed me off was the fact that he hadn't been up front with me about her. And then on top of that, his reaction toward me was like I was a flea or somethin'. I mean, had he told me he had somebody from the beginning, I woulda never said anything when I drove up and seen her in his truck. I woulda known what it was and kept it movin'. But he put me in a fucked-up position to have to find out some shit and be caught off guard.

I pulled up behind Nasir. He and the girl got out of his truck. I got out of my car as well.

"I'm goin' ask you one more time, and that's it, Nasir. *Who is this girl?*" she snapped. Her attitude and anger had gone up some notches since her first question about who I was.

"I told you a million times, Tara!"

"But not one of them times you told me the truth!" she accused. "Now what the fuck is it?"

"Fuck it, then," Nasir said, his attitude turning nonchalant, "Why don't you ask her?"

Meanwhile I was leaning against the passenger door of my car watching Nasir and the girl go back and forth, waiting for my turn to drill the nigga.

"Excuse me!" the girl turned around and started the short walk to me. "Who are you to Nasir?"

Before answering, I looked past her and glanced at him. He had a pitiful look on his face. And I actually felt bad for him in that brief moment. I took a few seconds to gather my composure, and I decided that I wasn't goin' to tell the girl the truth and hang Nasir no more than I already had done.

But before I spoke, Nasir hung himself and said, "Go 'head. You might as well tell her the truth now."

Then the girl just lost it. She turned around and ran up on Nasir, swinging on him again.

All the while she was screaming, "I KNEW IT! ALL THIS TIME! YOU FUCKIN' LIAR! I CAN'T BELIEVE YOU, NASIR!"

The girl was wailing on Nasir, hitting him in the face and everything. She was crying and screaming, just hysterical. I started feelin' bad for her at that point. I had been in her shoes before. I knew what pain she felt. And at the moment I wished I could have turned back the hands of time and erased everything that happened after I finished collectin' checks at the 7-Eleven.

Nasir finally grabbed hold of both the girl's hands and held them still. After a few attempts to break free she gave up. Still crying, she pretty much collapsed in his arms, burying her face in his chest. I approached them slowly, and said, "Look, for what it's worth, I'm sorry."

"Fuck you, Leah," Nasir said to me, cold.

I was confused, and my facial expression said so.

Nasir proceeded, still holding the girl close. "You ain't have to draw like you did. I mean, you got a dude! How you think I feel, every day you go home to that nigga, laugh and joke with 'im, eat dinner with 'im, and every night I know you layin' up with that nigga! You don't think that shit hurt? But I ain't never said shit! I ain't never put no pressure on you to give that up! And I damn sure ain't make it obvious to the nigga that we had our thing! And trust me, I had plenty opportunity, but naw, I let you do you! I let you keep ya home base! But you roll up on me on some jealous school-girl shit, causin' all this mayhem!" Nasir let me have it.

He was right about how he played his part throughout our short-lived relationship, but there was one thing he was wrong about, and I wanted him to know it and understand it. I wasn't lettin' him off the hook.

"That's all true, Nasir, but the difference is like you said, you knew all along I had a dude! You walked into this knowin' that! Me, on the other hand, I had no idea that you had a girl! It ain't like I ain't ask you! And you told me before you spend time or money on a girl it had to be somebody you planned on being with for a while or whatever! You remember that? You coulda told me right then and there I got somebody ya kna mean, and that woulda been that! This wouldn't be happenin' right now! But you didn't do that! You didn't keep it real with me!"

At that point the girl stopped crying and pulled away from Nasir. She stepped out of his arms and said, "I can't do this. Nasir, it's over. Miss, whatever ya name is, you can have 'im." Then she walked off.

"Let me take you to ya car, Tara," Nasir said, following behind her.

"No need!" she shouted back at him. "I can't stand to be in ya presence right now! I'd rather walk to my car!"

"Naw, come on, Tara!" he pleaded.

She put up her middle finger and kept walking.

He eventually stopped chasin' her and walked back down the street to where his truck was parked and where I was standing.

He shook his head at me and asked, "You happy?"

I nodded slowly, looking him in the eyes. "It's sad, and it may even be fucked up on my part, but yes, I'm very happy!"

Nasir leaned up against his truck and said, "You full of shit."

I walked over to him and took the spot that his girlfriend had just left. I wrapped my arms around his back and leaned my head against his chest. I squeezed him. And I said, "I think I'm in love with you, Nasir."

"Then why all the games? Huh? Why won't you leave Kenny today if you in love with me? Huh? What's keepin' you at bay? And don't talk that financial security shit to me. That counts for nothin' no more," he said.

I lifted my head up and looked at him. I wanted him to believe every word I was about to say. "I swear on my life if I could leave Kenny right now, I would. I woulda left him months ago if I could have—"

Nasir cut me off. "What's all this 'if I could have' shit? That's what I'm not understandin'! That's what's soundin' like game to me!" Nasir stood up straight and pulled his jeans up on his hips. Then he leaned against his truck once again. "All you gotta do is move ya feet and walk. I don't get you!"

"No, no," I began to explain. "It's not a matter of me just leavin' him! I can do that with no problem! But I got this case I'm fightin' with him right now. And if I leave him today or tomorrow, he goin' stop payment on my lawyer, and I'ma be left on my own tryna beat this thing with a public defender. It ain't about me and him! My freedom is on the line!"

"What a lawyer cost? Five stacks? All right, let's say I give you that. Would you leave the bull?"

I was silent for a minute as I thought about a way to explain my true dilemma to Nasir without giving away too much. I was even contemplating telling him the truth about my being an informant. But I had been told precisely not to let anybody know that I was a CI. Not even my family. All it took was for the information to get in the wrong hands and I could be discovered. I took that seriously, too, because that was the one thing I dreaded happening—being found out. That meant life or death to me. So I decided against telling Nasir after all.

"So I take that as a no," Nasir said, referring to his question about my leaving Kenny if Nasir would pay my lawyer tab.

"All right, listen," I said.

Nasir put his hands up and looked away. "Here come the bullshit," he mumbled.

"It's not bullshit!" I said.

Nasir grew aggravated. "It is, man! I don't understand why you just made that big-ass scene, fucked up shit between me and my girl . . . for what? What was the point?"

"You know what, you're right. I shouldn't have done that! I shoulda just let you be with ya girl. Go 'head. Be with ya girl. If that's what you wanna do," I said stubbornly, backing away from him, as if I was giving him permission to leave.

But instead of his leaving, he shot back, "No! See, that's where you wrong! I wanna be with you! That's where I wanna be! But you can't get that through ya head!" He poked me in my temple with his pointer finger. "You ain't tryna leave the bull! Every time I offer you a way out, you shoot it down! But you don't want me to be with nobody. You full of shit, man."

I was getting frustrated, wishing I could tell Nasir the real deal. I liked him so much. In fact, I had love for him. "Nasir, I need you to understand, it's not that I wanna be with Kenny! I don't! I just got a complicated situation goin' on and I need you to trust me when I say that! I wanna tell you the deal so, so bad, but it's a lot at stake!" I started getting emotional, and tears began to surface. "You think I go home every day with a smile on my face? You think I like layin' up with Kenny every night? Fuck no!" Tears fell down my face. "I hate Kenny! If you only knew what he did to me and if you only knew why I was still with him, this would be so simple right now! But it's not! It's complicated! And at the end of the day I'm the one carrying the most burdens around! And I'm not askin' you for sympathy! I'm a big girl. I got myself in this mess, and I'ma get myself out, God willing! All I'm askin' for from you is trust, understanding, and time. Trust that I got my reasons for stayin' with Kenny right now. Understand that I got a lot of shit I'm battlin' right now. And give me time to get to the finish. Once that happens, I'm free! I'm yours! I give you my word! I love you, Nasir! You been my rock through all of the shit I been goin' through, and you don't even know it! If you wasn't in my life right now, I'd probably be goin' crazy! That's why I know God put you in my life for a reason! I value you for that! And in due time I'll be able to show you. I just need you to ride it out with me until then," I poured.

Nasir didn't say anything. He just stared at me. Then he asked, "You love me?"

I nodded as I wiped my face with my hands.

"Naw, seriously, can you really say that you love me?"

"With all my heart," I said sincerely.

"Come here, man," he said, pulling me to him again. "I don't know what it is about you, Leah, but you got me. You do somethin' for me that no other girl has. And no matter how hard I try, I can't shake you."

"You tried to shake me?" I asked him in an innocent whisper.

He chuckled and said, "See. Just the little shit you say and do draw me to you. I don't know, man. I can't explain it." He took a breath and exhaled, then he said, "I'm goin' ride with you, Leah. Just don't end up hurtin' me, man. I'm puttin' a lot on the line for you. And I need it to be worth it in the end."

I lifted my head, reached up, and kissed Nasir on the lips. How he felt about me was unreal. Nothing short of magical. In his arms I felt like a princess who had been rescued by her Prince Charming. If only I was living a fairy tale.

Nasir

After my fight with Leah last week I realized just how much I felt for her. I wanted a serious relationship with her. No more sharing her with another nigga. She didn't know it, but I had plans for her to leave Kenny sooner than she thought.

I'd been grindin' hard, chasing all day and all night, tryin' to build a nice stash not only to hire Leah a lawyer to beat her case but also to be able to hold me and her down once she left Kenny.

I was seeing the fruits of my labor, too, when payday rolled around. Not only did I get three grand in commission from my pop, but I had a nice amount of money waiting for me at the lawyer's office and the medical center that day.

"Hi, how you doin', Cara? I have a ten o'clock appointment with Anthony," I told the woman at the front desk.

"Good morning, Nas. Have a seat. He'll be out shortly."

"Thanks," I said, walking over to one of the antique chairs that decorated the expansive reception area.

Anthony was the injury lawyer to whom I referred bodily injury cases. Basically, whenever I got a hit, not only did I refer the customers to my dad's shop to get their cars repaired, but I also referred them to Anthony to represent them in their lawsuits for medical and rehabilitation expenses. So just like I made a commission off people's cars, I also made a commission off their injury cases.

"Nas," Anthony greeted me with his hand extended for a shake. Then he joked, "Tell me something: is hip-hop dead or what?"

Although not funny, Anthony chuckled at his lame joke, which referred to the fact that my name was the same as Nas the rapper who two years ago had come out with an album titled *Hip-Hop Is Dead*. Anthony turned red and everything laughing at himself.

I just shook my head and smirked, "That's why middle-aged white men don't need to listen to rap music."

I followed Anthony to his corner office, almost jogging to keep up with his swift pace. I swear that nigga snorted coke. It had to be more than coffee that kept him so upbeat all the time.

"Have a seat," he said as we entered his office.

"So what's been goin' on? How was your Easter?" he asked, reaching into a bottom drawer on his desk. "Nice watch, by the way," he said, gazing at the diamond Audemars Piguet I had on. "Looks like I'm payin' you too much for these bodily injury cases." He chuckled.

I flagged him and said, "Aww, get outta here."

Anthony pulled a folded-up orange envelope from the drawer. He looked at the front of it first and mumbled, "Yup, Nas," then handed it to me. "Here's what I owe you for the four you brought me last week."

I took the envelope, opened it up, and peeked inside.

"It's four grand," Anthony said. "I'll give you what I owe you on the other three as soon as they go to therapy."

"Cool. I'll be signing them up this week."

"All right, well." Anthony stood up and patted me on the shoulder. "It's good doing business with you as always. Keep chasin' wrecks and bringing the injury cases my way, won't you? There's this yacht I wanna buy." He smiled.

I nodded and left his office. I walked down the hallway and saw myself back to the reception area. Cara was on the phone, so she couldn't verbally tell me to have a nice day. But she smiled and nodded at me as I headed toward the elevators. I returned the gesture.

I left Anthony's Center City law office and got my BMW 645 from the parking lot across the street. I didn't like driving my truck downtown. It was too much traffic, too busy. Plus, it was spring now, so I drove my car a lot more. For one, because I chased less, and for two, because it was a convertible—meant for warm, sunny days.

I drove to West Philly to the medical center to collect on the same BIs that Anthony had just paid me on. That was the beauty of bodily injury cases. A lawyer paid you a fee for each customer you sent his way to be represented by him in a lawsuit, and a doctor paid you a fee for each customer you sent his way for physical therapy. You didn't get paid just for the referral, though. You had to wait until the customer agreed and signed up to use the services. And then you had to wait until the customer actually went to therapy a few times before you got paid. Waiting was a way to give the doctors and lawyers assurance that the customers would be committed to going for physical therapy as often as needed, which meant their case would settle for more money, which in turn meant more money to the doctors and lawyers.

I went inside the small medical center, greeted the receptionist, and then met with the doctor in the back. He gave me $7,200, $1,800 per person since the insured had full tort. If the insured had had limited tort, I would have gotten less money, because limited-tort victims weren't covered for all injuries like full-tort victims were. Instead, they were covered only for extremely serious injuries, leading to little, if any, money damages at settlement.

I thanked Dr. Fresby and began to turn to walk away when he stopped me.

"Nas, I don't know if I told you, but some of the people you sign up show no evidence of having pain. I'll ask them if certain key areas hurt, and they'll say no. Now, I know that some of them aren't really accident victims but have been added to the police report after the fact. But they need to at least pretend like they were. One day they're gonna have to go to arbitration," he said. "They need to be coached."

"All right," I said. "That's a small thing." I tried easing Dr. Fresby's nerves. He was the type to worry more than he had to. But it was cool because I was the type to make him feel like he didn't have to.

"I'll coach 'em. I got you," I said, making a mental note to make sure all my customers knew to coach all of their friends or relatives who they would add on to the police report for the sake of gettin' them some case money.

"Okay, buddy," he said, walking me to the door. I waved good-bye to the receptionist and left the office.

I got in my car, blocked my number, and called Leah. After the first ring I hung up. If she was able to talk, she would call me back.

"Yo," I answered soon as she called me.

"What's up?"

"You in the mood to chase with me?" I asked her.

"I don't know," she said, sounding extra sexy. "What are you goin' give me if I do?"

"The ride of your life," I told her.

She laughed and then asked, "How can I resist?"

I arranged to pick her up from her mom's house, where she had been staying during the day since being fired from the shop a week ago.

She chased with me until about a quarter to five. And she turned out to be good luck for me, too, that day. I got two hits while I chased with her. I told her I would give her a couple dollars off the commission I'd make on them since she was keeping me company, making sitting in one place for hours listening to the constant chatter from police and medics over the scanners more fun and tolerable.

We had such a good time chasing together that we began to do it more often. Eventually, after a few days, it became our routine. Leah would leave her house every morning at eight, go to her mom's house to park her car, and I'd pick her up from there after rush hour at ten. She would chase with me and I would drop her back off at her mom's at about five, then she would go home from there.

It was as if she still worked at the shop. At least, that was what Kenny thought. And it worked out, too, because it gave Leah and me more time to spend together, and it allowed her to still make money as I broke her off whenever I got a hit while she was with me.

The only thing was, she still needed to present her paycheck to Kenny, which I didn't think was necessary, but apparently every Friday when she used to get paid she would give Kenny her check and he would deposit it for her and give her the cash. So she feared that if she stopped bringing him a check every week, he would find out that she didn't have a job anymore. So I agreed to help her out by having my pop pay me six hundred of every commission I got in a check and the rest in cash. My dad didn't suspect anything. I told him it was for tax purposes. I would then hand the check over to Leah so she could have something to show Kenny.

I felt bad about doing it, though, 'cause I ain't like lying to my pop about shit, especially not when it came to Leah and that nigga Kenny. My dad wasn't fond of me still involving myself with them, and he damn sure wouldn't have been with me givin' Leah one of his checks every week to keep up the facade that she still worked for him. Shit, he didn't even know Leah chased with me. So I had to be real secretive about a lot of things. And it was an internal struggle for me to mislead my pop like that, but I did it because, for one, I knew it was only temporary. And for two, and most importantly, I really wanted to help Leah.

Me of all people knew how it was to feel like you were stuck in a relationship with somebody. I dealt with that in my friendship with Kenny. If it was up to me I woulda been stopped bein' cool with that nigga. But he had dirt on me, and I couldn't help but feel like I had to be bothered with that nigga in order to keep that dirt buried. So I related to Leah and I wanted to help her get out of a sticky situation. Somehow, I felt that helping her would be helping me. Taking her from Kenny would be my way of finally standing up to that nigga and lettin' him know that he couldn't keep gettin' in the way of me livin' my life, being happy, and doin' the things I wanted to do, like how he brodied Leah from me in the first place. Call it revenge. Call me a sucker for love. Whatever the case, I was takin' back what was supposed to had been mine. I was goin' show that nigga.

Leah

I t was a Friday, the first one in May, and I had a lot on my plate. I was chasing with Nasir as usual and thinking about everything I had to do after he dropped me off at my mom's. I had to drive about twenty-five minutes from my mom's apartment on Seventy-fourth and Haverford Avenue to the 7-Eleven on Forty-second and Walnut Street to meet all the shop workers to collect their checks. Then from there I had a meeting with Detective Daily at a Starbucks way out Blue Bell, about forty miles away. He wanted to do a briefing with me, which he had begun to request more frequently.

And I was worried about going to this one because that morning when he called to set up our meeting, he stressed to me that I needed to start giving him more vital information. Apparently what I had been giving him he hadn't been able to prove and thus he couldn't make an arrest. He told me that the statute of limitations on my fraud charges were expiring really soon, and that if my information didn't lead to Kenny's arrest before the expiration date, my file would be turned over to the prosecutor and my case would be tried. I had been thinking about that all day, and it had me stressed.

"You all right?" Nasir asked as he pulled his truck over in front of my mom's complex. "You seem like you got a lot on ya mind today."

I nodded. "I'm cool. I'm just tired," I said somberly. "And I still gotta take my mom a couple places before I go home."

"Yeah, I know how ya Fridays be," Nasir said referring to the lie I told him about having to take my mom to her job to pick up her check every Friday. It was my excuse for having him drop me off earlier at my mom's on Fridays than the other days. I couldn't tell him that I actually had to meet his dad's employees.

I got out of his truck and walked toward the front door of the Copley Place, casually speaking to the various neighbors who were out on their balconies basking in the sun. Once inside the complex I took the elevator to the third floor and walked down the hall. I got to my mom's door and used the spare key she had given me to let myself in. My mom's job as a housekeeper at a nursing home required her to work overnight, so she usually slept in. So after two days of my coming to her house and knocking on her door at nine in the morning right after I lost my job, she decided she couldn't take it anymore and she gave me back my old key. That was fine by me. It allowed me to come and go as I pleased without disturbing her or relying on her to be there.

I walked in the door, prepared to say hi and good-bye to my mom and then walk right back out to go make all my runs. But my plans were abruptly changed when I saw that Kenny was standing in my mom's living room. I froze up with fear, especially when I saw that he was closing my mom's sliding-glass door as if he had just come in from her balcony. Had Kenny seen me get out of Nasir's truck? *Shit*, I thought. I instantly started trying to come up with something.

"Kenny?" I asked, stunned. "What are you doing here?"

Before he could say anything my mom spoke. "I told him you had stopped by here on ya lunch break and had went to the store for me. But he insisted he'd wait for you to come back," she said with attitude. She was sitting at the kitchen table smoking a cigarette and shaking her leg. She looked tired and was talking like she was short-tempered, like she was seconds away from cursing somebody out. I didn't know how long Kenny had been there waiting for me, but from the multiple cigarette butts that were in the ashtray in front of my mom, it looked like he'd been there stressin' my mom out for a while.

Kenny rubbed his face with the palm of his hand, then said to me, "I'm goin' give you five seconds to tell me why the fuck you just got out of Nas's truck and where you been for the last three hours."

I was caught completely off guard, and even though I didn't want to go along with my mother's lie that I had gone to the store for her, it seemed like my only option. My mind was blank. I couldn't think of anything else. But Kenny shut it down anyway.

"And don't say nothin' about no fuckin' lunch break, either, because when I drove by the shop earlier, the painter bull said you got fired from that mafucka! So where the fuck was you at? One, two, three . . ."

Okay, there went my alibi. I was scared stiff. It seemed like my mom's small living room was closing in on me.

"Four, five," Kenny finished. Then *pop*! He smacked me across my face.

At that my mom snapped. She stabbed her cigarette out in the ashtray in front of her and jumped up out her chair. "Hold the fuck up now!" She raised her voice, the scratchiness evidence of her habitual smoking. "I be goddamned if you think you goin' put ya hands on my daughter in my house!" she protested as she scrambled through a drawer and retrieved a medium-sized steak knife.

I looked at Kenny as my mom walked toward him bearing the knife. His face wrinkled up with intense fury. He looked like he was seconds away from seriously hurting somebody. I never saw him so mad before. The first thing I could think to do was stop my mom from approaching him. I rushed in front of her and started pushing her backward, careful not to cut myself.

"Ma, chill! Let me handle this!" I cried, trying to prevent an all-out war.

It was one thing for him to hit me, but if he had hit my mom I didn't know what was liable to happen. Somebody fucked around and ended up dead in that house.

My mom didn't challenge me and keep going at Kenny with the knife. However, she did continue to tell him off.

"Well, you cut his ass then, Leah! Shit, I'm tired of him thinkin' he can hit on you! And in my house? He must've lost his rabbit-ass mind!"

Kenny couldn't keep silent any longer. "Ms. Linda, you better listen to ya fuckin' daughter and chill!" he shouted over my mom's screaming. "You 'bout to get ya ass hurt for real!" Kenny warned, not at all threatened by my mom or the knife.

"What?" my mom persisted. "Motherfucker, I wish you would!"

"Ma, please!" I yelled, trying to contain my mother, who had started tryin' to attack Kenny again.

"You better chill! Matter of fact, you better get the fuck outta my house before I call the cops on ya punk ass! I'll tell 'em everything about you hustling drugs! See how long you can last in jail! You know you really a bitch! Only bitch-ass men put they hands on women!"

"Yeah?" Kenny tested. "Call the cops on me, and I'll burn this whole fuckin' buildin' down!" he retaliated.

"Kenny, just leave! Please!" I begged. "You don't need the trouble right now! Especially not over somethin' small!"

I was trying to say all the right things that would encourage Kenny to walk away from the fight. The longer the two of them went at it, the greater the chances were of a tragedy occurring. And that possibility scared me to death. So I tried to mediate as best I could.

"You know what, you right," Kenny concluded. "I don't need the trouble. Come on, Leah. We out," he said, turning toward the door, but not before grimacing at my mom.

"Leah, don't do it!" my mom said, giving Kenny the same look of disgust that he had given her. "Enough is enough," she said.

It pained me to have to walk out the apartment with Kenny after he had disrespected my mom to such a degree. But the fact of the matter was, I had to. I had only a short amount of time left to help the cops book Kenny, and if I didn't, I was headed to jail. I was stuck between a rock and a hard place—even worst, death and hell. And even though I desperately wanted to stay at my mom's and wash my hands of Kenny for good, I felt like I had no choice but to leave with him.

"Mom, I have to. I hope you understand. I love you and I don't wanna have to choose—"

"Leah, come the fuck on!" Kenny demanded from out in the hall.

My mom looked at me with tears in her eyes. She took a hard swallow and said, "I love you, too, Leah."

Then, as I was leaving the apartment, I heard my mom gasp, "Lord Jesus, protect my child!"

I closed the door and followed Kenny down the hall and onto the elevator. My heart was beating at an alarming rate. I had never felt so frightened in my life.

"Give me your car keys," Kenny ordered.

I dug in my pocketbook without reservation and grabbed my keys. I handed them over to Kenny.

"Press two," he said, as he took only my car key off the ring and then tossed the remaining keys back to me.

CHASER

I did what I was told. Kenny got off the elevator on the second floor and told me to hold the elevator doors open for him while he went to the apartment of one of his workers and gave the guy my car key.

After a few minutes Kenny returned to the elevator. "Sheen goin' get mad pussy drivin' his new car around," he mumbled to himself.

I took that as his way of tellin' me that he had given my car to one of his workers. And it didn't hurt me, either. I had bigger problems on my hand. I didn't know what Kenny was going to do to me. I had missed my meeting with the workers, and it looked as if I was going to miss my meeting with Detective Daily, too.

I followed Kenny out of the elevator, out the front door of the apartment building, and up the street to where his Suburban was parked. I was quiet the whole time, afraid to open my mouth about anything. He got in the driver's seat and I got in the passenger's seat. He started the SUV and pulled off.

Kenny didn't say anything more to me about my being dropped off by Nasir or about my having gotten fired without tellin' him. Although I knew he felt some type of way about all of it still. And that was what scared me. I didn't know how he was takin' it or when and how he planned to address it again. In the meantime, three days had gone by, and neither of us brought the subjects up. Matter of fact, we didn't do much speaking to each other about anything. Kenny had been staying out a lot, working, clubbing, and most likely spending time with his side chicks.

I just stayed in bed mostly, gettin' up only to eat, to use the bathroom, and to shower every night. I was depressed. I hadn't answered my phone all weekend, not for Nasir, my mom, none of the workers at the shop, and not even Detective Daily. I didn't even check my messages until that Tuesday morning.

The first message was from Detective Daily; *"Leah, you pulled a no-show on me. What's goin' on? Call me ASAP. I need a status on you."*

The second one was from Joe, the painter. *"Hey, Leah, it's Joe. Joe Parker. Listen, um, I was wonderin' if you was goin' come through with that money like we been doin' because I lost my ID and can't cash my check. I was kind of depending on you Friday. What happened? Please call me because I need to get my check cashed. Thanks. 'Bye."*

Then there was a message from Nasir, except he didn't say anything. I knew it was him, though, because I heard scanners in the background.

The last message was from my mom. *"Leah, where are you? Answer ya phone. That guy Nasir been by here for you this morning. I didn't tell him what happened, but maybe you should. Maybe he can kick Kenny's ass for you. He seems like a nice guy. And it's obvious you two like each other. Why don't you leave Kenny's sorry ass while you can. And give that nice guy Nasir a chance. Call me. Let me know you're all right."*

I hung up my phone, and the only person I called back was the detective. He didn't answer his phone, so I left him a message. I simply stated, "Hi, it's Leah. I am sorry for missing our meeting. An emergency came up. Call me to reschedule, please."

I ended the call and lay back down in my bed. I wanted to cry, but I didn't feel any tears. I guessed I was all cried out.

Nasir

hadn't spoken to Leah since I dropped her off at her mom's almost a week ago. I was a little worried because she seemed out of it that day, like she wasn't herself. I hoped she was all right.

I was at the barbershop sitting in the chair gettin' a shape-up when I got a call from a blocked number. I answered it quickly, thinking it was Leah.

"Hello."

"Nas," my dad's voice sounded, disappointing me. "Where you at?"

"The barbershop," I said.

"Well, soon as you get done, I need you to meet me at the shop. I need to talk to you about somethin', but not over the phone," he said with a mixture of urgency and anger in his tone. "Hurry up, though," he added, then hung up.

My barber, Mel, finished me up. I paid him and then got in my truck and headed to the shop. Brock was in the passenger's-side seat waiting for me. I had been lettin' him chase with me those few days that Leah was MIA. He had been doin' good listenin' to the scanners, being able to make out what the dispatchers were saying through all the static, and he was starting to learn the different codes that some of the dispatchers used to describe accidents, like MVA, instead of just saying "auto accident" like they normally did. So I trusted him to sit in the truck and be my ears while I was in the barbershop.

"Where you drivin' to all fast?" he asked. "Ain't no accident come out. I been listenin'."

"Naw, I know. I gotta go to the shop real quick. My pop wanna holla at me," I told him.

"Oh. What's wrong?" Brock asked.

"I don't know. He sounded like he was mad though."

"All shit," Brock said. "TGIAF."

"What? Fuck that mean?"

"Thank God it ain't Friday," he explained. "Get that nigga mad on a Friday, and he mess around and don't pay nobody. And I don't need that kinda drama right now. A nigga gotta pay rent."

"Pay rent to who, ya grandmom? Don't you still live in her basement?" I laughed.

Brock played cool. "Yeah, but it's decked out, though. It's like my own little apartment down there. Got a bathroom, a TV, a mattress. Everything I need. And shit, long as the chicks dig it, I'm cool."

"What chicks? Chicks don't dig bein' in nobody's basement on no mattress, dog. Especially not at ya age," I teased him. "You thirty years old."

"Age ain't nothin' but a number, my nigga," Brock said. Then he started rubbing his face. "Plus, I got this smooth baby face, nigga. The girls think I'm still in high school."

That was true, too. Brock didn't have any facial hair, with the exception of a light-ass mustache. I could believe it when he said girls thought he was still in high school.

"Unlike you," Brock went on, "who look like somebody's old-ass sugar daddy."

I chuckled and continued to be entertained by Brock as I weaved in and out of the traffic heading to the shop. Brock had me laughin' the whole way. He was a natural comedian. That was why I fucked with him heavy. He was the coolest dude you could meet, always smilin' and laughin', even when shit wasn't goin' his way. He was the type of dude you would never see mad. Life was just funny to that nigga. So no matter what obstacles he faced, like not being able to read and write, and having been abandoned by his mom and dad when he was a kid, he always seemed to be the happiest dude on the planet. That was why, out of all the guys who worked at my dad's shop, I clicked with him the most. He was just a positive person. He was my homie.

I pulled up to the shop and threw the truck in park. On my way out, I turned to Brock.

"I'ma need you to hold it down for me while I see what my pop want. It might be a little slow now with the morning rush hour almost over, but don't be discouraged. You just gotta ride it out, 'cause ever so often somethin' come out and you can get it because you the only nigga that stayed out during the dry period. All the other niggas go in," I schooled Brock.

"I'm cool, though. I can stay out all day long as I can play the PlayStation. Man, that's the best thing you could've put in ya truck."

"It was either that or get a daily blow job to keep me still," I told him.

"Well, I think you made the right choice. A blow job only lasts about five minutes. You would be ready to roll after that."

I laughed and said, "Nigga, you funny at breakfast."

At that moment the scanner produced a long and steady beep,

which usually preceded a call to an accident. Brock and I both grew quiet as we listened for the dispatcher to announce the emergency.

"*Medic Nine, Four-seven and Baltimore . . .*" the female voice said.

"You heard that?" I asked Brock.

"Yup. Four-seven and Baltimore," he repeated.

Then the voice came back: "*Robbery victim shot in abdomen. Suspect a black male wearing dark blue Dickies and a navy baseball cap headed south on Baltimore on foot.*"

"Damn," Brock said, "I'd rather be funny at breakfast than shot at breakfast. Niggas be wilin' early in the morning."

"You stupid, man," I said as I got out of the truck. "I'll call you when I need you to come pick me up."

"All right," Brock said, getting out of the passenger's side and walking around to the driver's seat.

I walked in the shop and sensed an eerie feeling right away. I spoke to Frank, the parts manager, who was organizing a bunch of different parts on a shelf. Then I said what's up to Joe Porter and the rest of the workers. They all said what's up back, but none of them had a joke. None of them asked me to hold a couple dollars. None of them had an outrageous story to tell me. Nothin'. They all seemed like they had lost a loved one. I wondered what I was walkin' into.

I went in my dad's office, and he had a bunch of papers laid out on his desk. He wasn't frowning or nothin', but he looked upset.

"Shut the door," he instructed.

"What's up?" I asked, following his instructions.

"Yo, you know anything about Leah washing my checks?"

Immediately, I thought about how I had been giving Leah checks every Friday, and my defenses went up. I couldn't let that be known, especially not now while there seemed to be a problem. "Naw! What you mean?" I dumbed down.

"I mean, like taking checks that I write out to people and changing them to be made payable to mafuckas she know."

"I know what washing checks means. But I don't know nothin' about Leah doin' that."

"You sure?"

"I'm positive. Why, what happened?"

"Well, recently I had moved some money around, and a check I wrote bounced. I had ya mom pull up the account online to see which check it was, and it was made out to somebody I ain't know. So I looked into it and found a bunch of payroll checks that I had wrote out to my employees that ended up being rewritten to other mafuckas who I ain't never hear of. So I started askin' questions around this mafucka, and eventually I got some answers. What she been doin' was takin' everybody's paychecks every Friday, washing them, and depositing them in bank accounts that belong to other businesses or people. Like this one," he said, holding up a computer printout of a cashed check. "I wrote this check out to Joseph Parker—"

"The painter? Joe?" I clarified.

"Yeah," my dad said. "But she gave Joe cash and took his check, erased my writing, and wrote it out to whoever she wanted to, basically usin' my check to pay other people for shit like plumbing services, construction work, interior design, property management, all this shit." My dad was rummaging through the many printouts of checks. "The bitch is slick."

I got a little shook up. I didn't want my dad to find out that I had been a participant in what was looking like a scam against him. First of all, that wasn't the case. I never intended to scam my pop. I would have never been down for no shit like that. I mean, granted, I was wrong for goin' behind his back with the shit that I had done, but it was not on some scandalous shit like what my dad was revealing to me. I needed to get to the bottom of what Leah had goin' on and the scope of what she had possibly involved me in.

"I don't get it, though," I said, trying to wrap my head around what my dad was suggesting of Leah. "If she had the money to give Joe and everybody else, why wouldn't she just use it to pay all the people you say she paid with the checks? Why would she need people's checks at all? I don't see the point. Maybe Joe and everybody is throwin' her in the fire to cover their own ass, and maybe they chose to blame Leah because she's the only one not here anymore to defend herself." I didn't want to believe for one second that Leah would fraud my pop. Not my pop. I mean, she might have been capable of doin' her share of dirt, especially with a nigga like Kenny in her ear. But I refused to believe that she was capable of crossing me or my mothafuckin' family.

"Naw," my dad disagreed. "None of these niggas are sophisticated enough to have been able to pull off nothin' like this. That's number one. Plus, don't none of them have the money to cash nobody's checks."

"True," I mumbled. As hard as it was for me to face, my dad was right.

"It had to be Leah, dog. She was usin' me to clean that nigga Kenny's money up," my dad concluded. "I told you she was fuckin' trouble. Didn't I say it?"

I nodded, then went deep into thought. "But that's crazy, though," I said. "What was she thinkin'?"

"Yo, get her on the phone right now," my dad demanded.

Without hesitation I dialed Leah's cell. There was no answer, like I figured. Ever since I dropped her off that past Friday, she hadn't been answerin' any of my calls or callin' me. I went to redial her from the shop phone just to see if she would pick up then.

"Naw," my dad stopped me. "Don't even worry about it. I ain't goin' ask her shit. Joe said she still be meetin' them after work on Fridays to switch off. So this Friday I'm goin' go to the 7-Eleven where she meet everybody at, I'm goin' catch her ass in the act," my dad concluded.

CHASER

On that note, my dad told me that if I spoke to Leah between then and Friday, not to say anything to her about the checks. He didn't want her to be tipped off.

I gave him my word that I wouldn't warn her, but deep down I wanted to. I wanted to ask her straight up if she had done what my dad's workers had said she'd done. But shit, she wasn't even answerin' my calls, so I couldn't ask her shit if I wanted to. And it was eatin' at me, too. I started thinking that maybe that was the reason she had been duckin' me. Maybe she got wind of the fact that she had been exposed. Whatever the case may be, I was anxious to find out the truth. I found myself counting down the three days until Friday.

It was prom season, so over the past week limos, gowns, and suits had flooded the streets. It seemed like every time I turned around, somebody I knew little sister or cousin was goin' on a prom. And on that particular Friday I had like five people to see off between seven and nine. But first and foremost, I had to go with my dad to the 7-Eleven to see what the hell was goin' on with Leah.

We were in my dad's Yukon. We didn't want Leah to see my truck or my dad's truck and get scared and leave. It felt like we were on a stakeout.

"I swear on everything if this shit go down, all them niggas is fired. And that bitch, oh man, I got some plans for her ass, too," my dad said, spazzin'.

I wasn't mad like my dad, not yet anyway. I really was hopin' that we were wastin' our time out there. I hoped Leah wouldn't show. I didn't want that shit about her to be true.

My heart was starting to beat faster as the clock crept up to five fifteen, the time Leah was expected to pull up into the parking lot. I was looking out the side mirrors to see if I could spot her. There was no sign of her, and I started to feel anxious. I willed the clock to fly past 5:15 and for Leah not to show. I wanted more than anything for it all to be one big misunderstanding.

Then my dad sat up in the driver's seat and adjusted the rearview mirror. "I think this is her," he said.

A gray Maserati, the same color as Kenny's, pulled into a parking space two cars away from where my dad and I were parked. It was Kenny and Leah. Kenny was driving. Leah was in the passenger's seat. Once parked, neither of them got out of the car. Instead, they waited while Leah made a phone call on her cell. Seconds later, a scared-looking Joe walked out of the store. He glanced over at my dad and me and twitched his eyes, lookin' real suspicious. He walked over to Leah's car. As they were exchanging something, my dad and I walked up on them.

"Get the fuck out the car, man!" my dad instructed Kenny. Then he turned his attention to Joe. "Yo, Joe, give that mafuckin' money up. Nasir, get that shit from 'im."

At that point Joe handed me the cash Leah had given him. He started apologizing and beggin' my dad for forgiveness, talkin' about he didn't know what Leah was doin' with the checks. My dad wasn't tryin' to hear none of that shit, though. He told him he'd better leave now while he still had legs to do so. Joe took off running out of the parking lot and around the corner.

Meanwhile, Leah's face looked like she had just seen a ghost. She had one hand over her heart and everything.

"Fuck is you doin', man?" I snarled at her, not able to withhold my anger toward her.

"Get them fuckin' checks from her, Nas!" my dad said. Then he turned back to Kenny, who remained in the car with a smirk on his face while he sipped on a supersized McDonald's drink.

"Niggga, you heard what the fuck I said! Get out the mafuckin' car! I know it was you who put her up to this shit!" My dad approached the driver's side, where Kenny was sitting.

"Whatchu talkin' 'bout?" Kenny asked with arrogance.

My dad then opened the door himself and gripped Kenny up out the car. At that Kenny threw his drink on my dad and swung on him at the same time. My dad didn't swing back, but he pulled out his pistol and cracked Kenny across the face with it.

Leah screamed and started crying as she fiddled to open the glove compartment and retrieve two checks. Her hand shaking, she handed the checks to me, practically throwing them at me.

I quickly glanced at the checks and started to stuff them in my pocket when I had to take a second look at them. One was made out to me, dated for last Friday, the day I had dropped Leah off at her mom's, then hadn't heard from her again. I put that one in a separate pocket from the one that was made out to Joe. I had to remember which pocket I put which check in because I didn't want to run the risk of giving my dad the check that was made out to me. That would have put me in the same category as Joe and them other niggas—sheisty. And even though my reasons for giving her checks were different from the others', my dad wouldn't have seen it that way. Goin' behind his back was goin' behind his back. Disloyalty was disloyalty.

My dad had Kenny pinned up against the Maserati. And I could see that my dad was ready to hit him again. That's when I rushed over to stop him, and not for Kenny's sake either, 'cause truth be told, I wanted to fuck him up myself. I heard sirens, and I didn't want my pop goin' to jail, especially not for no-nut-ass nigga like Kenny.

I pushed my dad toward his car. In the meantime, Leah had gotten out of the car. She was still crying, pleading for the commotion to stop.

"I'm sorry! Please stop!" she sobbed to my dad and me.

"LEAH, COME THE FUCK ON, 'FORE YOU GET LEFT!" Kenny shouted, as he scurried into his car. "FUCK YOU CHASIN' AFTER THAT NIGGA FOR?"

But Leah didn't take heed. Instead, she completely ignored Kenny.

At that, Kenny put the car in reverse, and as he was speeding out the parking lot he was shouting, "WAIT RIGHT HERE, MUTHA-FUCKA! I GOT SOMETHIN' FOR YA ASS! BOTH OF Y'ALL NIGGAS!"

"ALL NIGGA, YOU AIN'T GOT SHIT!" my dad shot down Kenny's threats.

"LEAH, YOU'S A DEAD BITCH, TOO!" were Kenny's last words before he sped out of the parking lot and disappeared into the traffic.

Leah didn't respond to him. She didn't even react to being left. She was more focused on pleading her case to me. She was crying like a battered woman. Her eyes looked weary. She even looked like she had lost some weight since I seen her last. I wanted to feel empathy for her, but I couldn't. She had betrayed me, and there was no comin' back from that.

"You hate me, Nasir? Don't hate me, please," she cried, reading my facial expression correctly.

"What the fuck you expect, Leah? You was scammin' my pop! Takin' his checks and washin' that nigga's money who got you out here lookin' like a fuckin' nut! When you goin' learn, Leah? Huh? Why you keep allowin' yaself to be in fucked-up situations for the bull? Are you really over him? Huh? Or do you love that nigga that much?"

"I didn't want to do it. I swear, I didn't. But that damn Kenny. He made me do it. And you, Nasir, of all people know that it's not easy tellin' him no sometimes." She wept.

She was right about that. I knew how Kenny was. But that wasn't goin' fly that time. The only reason why he had me by the balls was because he actually had dirt on me. But what did he have on Leah that was so bad that he could control her like he did? She kept sayin' she had her reasons for stayin' an all that, but what were they? I needed to know.

"Nas, we gotta go. Fuck her!" my dad shouted out as he walked toward his SUV.

"Mr. Vic, you don't understand! I never wanted to do that to y'all! I swear to God on my life!" she cried out to my dad.

My dad shook his head at Leah and said, "Don't cry now. It's more to come, baby. You don't know what you let that nigga get you into."

I thought about the threat my dad posed on Leah. Taking a step toward her, I said, "You put yaself on the line for this nigga, and he had the audacity to leave you out here in this parking lot with my pop while my pop is on fire ready to kill somebody. He don't fuckin' love you. He don't even care about you. So tell me somethin', Leah, and I want the truth this time: Why is it so hard for you to leave this nigga alone?"

"Nas! Let's go!" My dad pulled the Yukon up to where Kenny's car had been parked, where Leah and I were talking.

My eyes stuck on Leah, I told my pop, "Dad, go 'head. I'ma get up with you later."

"What? What are you doin'?"

I turned away from Leah and looked at my dad. "I need answers, Dad. For myself. I need answers."

My dad gave me a crazy look and frowned. "Nigga, if you don't get in this mafuckin' car!" he ordered.

"I can't. I want to. Trust me, I'm mad as shit at her. But I just need a minute with her," I tried to explain.

With a disgusted look on his face, my dad shook his head, backed the SUV up, and whipped it out of the parking space. He stopped and said, "Go 'head. But give me my keys."

"What keys?"

"My keys to *my* truck that ya ass make a livin' drivin'!"

"So you goin' take me out of the truck?"

"I can't trust you, dog. And that's fucked up 'cause you my oldest son. You supposed to be my right-hand man."

The cops were at the light now, obviously on their way into the lot. For that reason, I didn't want to hold my dad up any longer. I took my truck key off my key ring and tossed it to him. He sped off, looking like he had more anger for me than for Kenny and Leah put together. I felt fucked up about it, too. But I needed to resolve things with Leah. I knew her differently than my dad did, and I needed to know her motives behind the shit she'd done before I could just write her off. Of course, that would be hard for my dad to understand, because he was right. I was his oldest son, and for years I had been his right-hand man, following his lead without question. But this time was different. I had to follow my heart on this one. I needed closure.

"So what is it, Leah?"

"I got a few more weeks left before I can leave Kenny," she said slowly and nervously. She was twiddling her fingers and looking all around. I wasn't used to seeing her so unstable. It was breaking my heart to see how beat down she was.

"Why a few weeks? Why not right the fuck now? And be frank with me, Leah! Don't be beatin' around the bush and all that shit like you usually do!"

"I know it's hard for you to understand, Nasir. But if I could leave Kenny today, I would!"

"I heard that before, but what you ain't tellin' me is, *Why not?* And this time before I walk outta ya life for good and possibly never see you again, I need you tell me why not! Lawyer fees?" I pulled a knot of money out of my pocket and held it up in Leah's face. "I got that! A place to live? I got a crib—comfortable one, too! Financial stability? You can work! You ain't handicapped! So tell me, Leah, if it ain't the fact that you in love with this nigga, what is it?"

Leah shook her head but didn't respond.

CHASER

I snapped, "You played me, man!" I said, pounding my fist into the palm of my hand. "I lost my girl 'cause of you; my fuckin' pop is mad at me 'cause of you. I even had to give up my truck! Everything! Since this bullshit between me and you started, I've been the one bending over backward for you, Leah! And the one nigga I ask you to give up, which is the same nigga that's whippin' on ya ass, cheatin' on you every chance he get, puttin' you in positions to get locked up— and you can't do it! But yet you can rip my pop off! Scam me into givin' you checks! What if my pop find that shit out? You know how that's goin' look after all this? I fuck around and lose my family fuckin' with you!" I shook my head in shame. "You ain't shit, Leah! Fuck you!" I walked past her to leave the parking lot. She grabbed my arm and stopped me.

"Wait!" she said, "I'll tell you." Her lips quivering, she whispered, "I'm an informant tryin' to get Kenny locked up."

I smirked and said, "That's a good one. That another one of ya scams? Just say it: you played me. And now you just makin' up anything to get me back on ya side. Man, get the fuck outta here," I said, shrugging my arm out of her hand.

"I'm not lyin', Nasir! That's the truth! This whole time that's what it's been, and I couldn't tell you because it was against protocol! I couldn't tell anybody! I had to carry that shit on me all by myself!" Leah lowered her voice. "That's why I even did the check thing, Nasir, because I knew it was no way for ya dad to get caught up in that shit. I was the one givin' the cops information, and I knew what to tell them and what not to tell them. And I damn sure wasn't tellin' them nothin' that would incriminate you or ya dad or me! Only shit on Kenny! And that's why I stay. Because I have to report on him, or I'll go to jail! And it ain't been easy! It's been stressin' the shit out me! I want it to end! I want it to be over! Nasir, I wanna be done with Kenny! I do! I wanna be with you more than anything in this world!" Leah broke down.

Somehow I couldn't feel sorry for her. I mean, I wanted to, bad. But I didn't. The truth was, I just couldn't believe a word she said. Not at that point I couldn't. Maybe she should have told me all that sooner. Maybe things woulda ended differently. She waited too late. She had already lost my trust. And I couldn't take the chance of trusting her again. I left Leah where she was. I didn't respond to her pleas for me to come back. I flagged her and kept it movin'. I walked down Walnut Street and called one of my dad's other chasers to come pick me up. *Bitches ain't shit*, I thought.

Leah

Detective Daily," I cried into the phone. "I can't do this anymore! Just come lock me up and do what y'all gotta do! I can't be with this nigga no more! Fuck this shit! Just give me that fraud charge! Fuck it. Give me the time! It can't be worst than the shit I'm goin' through with Kenny! Please, just come lock me the fuck up!" I was having a fit outside on the curb in front of the 7-Eleven.

"Calm down, Ms. Baker. I can't make out what you're saying. Get yourself together, first, then explain to me what's goin' on."

I fought back tears and took a moment to gather my composure. "How much longer do I have to do this? How much more stress and how many more lies?"

"Ms. Baker, listen to me. We want him caught as bad as you. It's just that we need something concrete on this guy, or he's likely to walk. The leads you've been giving us have been helpful but not enough. We need you to hang in there, and not just for us but for your own good. At the end of the month we have to turn your file over to the prosecutors. Try hard, Ms. Baker, to give us something by then."

I broke down in tears again. "How? What am I supposed to do? I've done all I could! I've given you everything you've asked for! What more do y'all want from me?"

"Stop hollering. You have got to grab ahold of yourself, or you could compromise this whole deal," the detective told me. "Let's meet," he said. "I'll tell you what you need to do."

I agreed to meet the detective at the Tabernacle Lutheran Church on Fifty-eighth and Spruce. We hung up, and my next call was to a cab company.

Nasir

For the last two weeks I had been chasing with a couple of my dad's other guys while he was still trippin' about my havin' my truck. And I felt like I was in a lose-lose situation, because it wasn't like I had gotten anywhere with Leah. I was still hurt and infuriated with her. So I had my pop mad at me for nothin', basically.

"Yo, you out?" I had called Brock on his cell. My dad had put him in my truck in my place, and he had been chasin' full-time.

It was a rainy Memorial Day weekend. The kind of day I would have died to be out chasin'. First of all, rainy days tended to produce the most accidents; second of all, it was Memorial Day weekend, which meant the streets were bound to be packed with drivers. Not to mention some drunk drivers. Don't get me wrong, I didn't prey on the weak, nor did I wish accidents on people. But it was what it was. Accidents were goin' to happen whether I was a wreck chaser or not.

Plus, the way I looked at it, I actually helped people. Most times I was on the scene of a hit before the cops even got there. So I was able to calm the victims down, talk to them while they waited for the police and medic, and offer some sort of support and comfort. On top of that, I was helpful to the police: I was the one who would often clean the glass out the street and tow the car out of the way to get the traffic moving. So it wasn't like I was just this money-hungry nigga who took advantage of people. I was just doing a job like any other grown-ass man who had to take care of himself.

"And you know this, maaan," Brock imitated Chris Tucker in the movie *Friday*.

"Won't you come grab me? I don't wanna chase out my car in the rain."

"Shit, I don't know why ya ass chase out that pretty mafucker at all."

"I know. I'm 'bout to get a squatter until I find another shop to put me in a truck."

"Won't you take some of that money and buy ya own truck? Stop hustlin' backward, nigga."

"Either way, whatever shop I bring work to is goin' have to pay my note, so I still gotta find a home base. Plus, nigga, ain't nobody hustlin' backward."

"You and ya pop need to squash y'all beef anyway."

"You sound like my mom and shit."

My conversation with Brock was interrupted by the scanner.

Beeeeep . . . *"Medic Nine, Five-six and Girard."*

"Run that," I butted in.

"I'm 'bout to," Brock said with urgency. "I just gotta wrap this game up."

"Auto-ped," the dispatcher continued.

CHASER

"Oh, it's a auto-ped," Brock repeated, the urgency in his voice gone.

"You know what a auto-ped is?" I gave Brock a pop quiz.

"It's when somebody got hit by a car," he answered correctly.

"Do you know why they call it a auto-ped?" I really was testing him.

" 'Cause it's a auto versus a pedestrian, so for short it's a auto-ped. Nigga, I got this!" he boasted.

"You do. I gotta give it to you. I'm impressed a little bit. But you still need help out on those streets. Plus, I feel like whippin' ya ass in Madden. Come get me."

"All right, I'm on my way. Be ready, nigga," Brock said. "And bring some paper with you, 'cause I got my dice on me."

"All nigga, you ain't sayin' nothin'. My money lookin' for some friends, nigga."

"All shit, here you go," Brock said, "And don't be bitchin' about goin' home either, 'cause I plan on bein' on these streets all night."

"Nigga, I was bred on the streets. I know about all-nighters. How the fuck you think I made a name for myself? Sleepin' in? Fuck no. You talkin' to the king of these streets, pussy."

"Yeah?"

"Hell yeah!"

"Then why the king ain't got no truck?"

"Fuck you, nigga."

Brock got a laugh in and then we hung up. Soon as we did I noticed I had a text message from Leah. It said to call her—emergency. But I resisted. She was probably just hollerin' at me 'cause Kenny was out spending the holiday with another broad. I wasn't nobody's rebound nigga. I ain't feel like being bothered with that shit.

Leah

At the meeting I had with Detective Daily a couple weeks ago he gave me just the pep talk I needed to regain control in my situation. He let me know pertinent information about a deal Kenny had coming up that could possibly be the transaction to send him away. Apparently, he had other sources informing on Kenny, but they weren't as close to him as I was, so they got only limited details. They told Detective Daily about the deal, but they couldn't give him when and where it was supposed to go down. That was where I came in. I was to get those crucial details. And from what I had observed from Kenny that day I believed something was going down that night.

His brother Tim had been over earlier. They had put bags upon bags of packaged cocaine in the trunk of Kenny's Impala. And I overheard them talking about meeting up later. Plus, Kenny's phone had been ringing off the hook that whole day. I was almost certain the deal the detective had told me about was taking place that night. I just had to get the facts.

I was in the bathroom and just finished sending Nasir a text message when Kenny barged in. Startled, I dropped my phone on the marble floor. It was a good thing the battery came out when it fell or else Kenny would have been able to read Nasir's reply, if he had sent one. He hadn't been returning my calls or text messages. I assumed he still was not willing to believe what I had told him. It was nerve-wracking, but I wasn't going to give up on Nasir. I truly had love for him, and I was willing to prove it.

"Shit, you scared me," I mumbled, picking up the pieces of my phone.

"My bad," he said. "Hurry up, though, I gotta piss."

I got up and pulled up my pants. I stepped away from the toilet so that Kenny could use it. I was looking at myself in the mirror as I washed my hands. It was then that I decided to start acting on my plan. I took a deep breath and I said, "Listen, let's go to dinner."

"Dinner?" Kenny asked.

"Yeah, the meal that people eat in the evening," I said, trying to use sarcasm to ease the tension that had been between us for some time.

"I know what dinner is," he said, still grumpy. "I can't, though. I'm goin' to one of my boys' cookouts."

"Well, how about I go with you?" I suggested in a sweet, inviting tone, trying to be seductive and keep my nerves relaxed at the same time. I turned Kenny around to face me as he put his penis in his boxers, then pressed up against him.

"What's all this?" he asked, not resisting my grinding on him.

"It's my peace offering," I said, making my way down on my knees.

"We haven't talked in a while, Kenny. Yet we been havin' a lot of issues. I think it's time we clear everything up and try to resolve whatever grudges we got against each other." I slid his penis back out of his boxers.

"Yeah, well, all that shit is in the past," Kenny said as he placed one of his hands on the top of my head.

I reluctantly licked the tip of Kenny's dick. Then I continued, "Yeah, but I wanna clear the air." I licked it again and said, "The only reason I was in Nasir's truck that day was because the detectives had been pressurin' me to get more information on him. They orchestrated me gettin' fired so that I could chase with Nasir and find out which lawyers and doctors he dealt with," I lied.

"Yeah?" he asked, seemingly uninterested. "Why you ain't tell me that shit then?" He surprised me.

I licked his dick again, then gave it a few sucks, too. "I didn't want you to worry about me bein' in the truck with Nasir. I didn't want you to be insecure over nothin'." I went back to sucking his dick.

Kenny didn't say anything in response. He just moaned at the action I was giving him. I had managed to psyche myself out for the remainder of Kenny's blow job, closing my eyes and imagining he was Nasir. I got so caught up in my thoughts that tears came to my eyes. I missed Nasir. I missed the happiness he brought to me. I missed having sex with him, too. I wondered if he'd ever find it in his heart to forgive me.

Once I felt Kenny getting close to climaxing, I slipped his dick out of my mouth. "Stay home with me. Don't go to the cookout. It's raining outside anyway," I said.

"I can't," he said. "Now put my dick back in ya mouth." He guided my head back toward his bulging penis.

I licked it a couple times, but I didn't want to make him cum. Not until I got what I needed out of him.

CHASER

"Why not, Kenny? Why can't you keep it in tonight? We could watch movies and cuddle like we used to. I wanna get back what we had once upon a time."

Kenny began to frown, frustrated. "Leah, I can't tonight."

I licked him again.

"Umm," he moaned.

"Why not, Kenny? You got plans with ya other girl?"

"Come on, man," he said, losing patience.

"Then what is it, Kenny?" I pulled away from him.

"I got a meeting tonight," he said.

"Where at?" I probed.

"Why you askin' me all these questions?" he said, aggravated.

My heart started to pound as I wondered if I had made it too obvious that I was trying to get information out of him. I was scared, but I couldn't falter. It was time for me to step it up. I had to go all the way to get more information. This was the break I needed. It was now or never.

"Because I don't believe you, that's why, Kenny." I began to cry. "You been practically living with another girl for the last three weeks!" I made it about my being jealous rather than about my prying for info. I stood up and added, "You're hardly here! You come, eat, grab some clothes, and leave."

"What you doin'?" Kenny asked. "Finish what you started and stop trippin'." He closed the toilet seat and sat down on it. Then he grabbed my arm and pulled me close to him again.

He moved my hair out of my face gently and aligned his dick with my mouth. "I ain't goin' do nothin' on you tonight, man. I ain't thinkin' about no pussy. I got a million-dollar deal on the table tonight. Other niggas might be out partyin' and lookin' for freaks, but not me. Only place I'm focused on bein' is at the Belmont Plateau at one o'clock sharp," he broke. "So you ain't got shit to worry about. Now, finish makin' ya man feel good. Help me get relaxed."

MIASHA

I finished the deed, then allowed Kenny to relieve himself. All the while I was filled with anxiety. I couldn't wait for him to be gone.

It was close to midnight when Kenny finally left. Immediately I got on the phone and called Detective Daily.

"I have the information you were looking for," I blurted out.

"Whatchu got?" he asked, excitement in his tone.

"He's making the transaction tonight. It's supposed to be a million-dollar deal."

"When and where?" he asked.

"The Belmont Plateau at one."

"Okay. I gotta make some calls. I'm on it," Detective Daily said, rushing his words. "Good job, kiddo."

When I hung up I was feeling jittery. I couldn't sit down. I paced the bedroom and bit my nails. I needed someone to talk to. I tried calling Nasir, but I didn't get an answer. I called him right back one last time and that time I was forwarded to his voice mail.

I sat down on my bed, my head in the palms of my hands. *Damn it,* I thought. *I really fucked up with Nasir.*

Nasir

Snake eyes!" Brock called out as he let the dice tumble out of his palms.

"Seven, eleven!" I tried to jinx him.

"Damnit," he said. "I keep comin' close," he referred to the two and the one that appeared on the dice.

He picked the dice up and shook them up in his hand again, but before he rolled, a long beep sounded from the scanner. We both paused and listened intently to what was about to be called.

"Medic Nine, One-four-four-two North Felton Street. Domestic dispute. Female complaintiff. One-four-four-two North Felton Street."

"It's been a lot of domestic disputes," Brock said. "Niggas' girls probably givin' them hell about goin' down Miami to South Beach. They get to arguin' and the shit probably hit the fan," he theorized.

"Nigga, just shoot the dice and crap out so I can get on them things and show you how money get made."

Brock shook the dice up again, getting his head back into the game. And just as he was about to roll, he was distracted for the second time. This time it was by my phone ringing. I looked at the screen and pressed ignore.

"Who the hell you duckin'?" Brock asked me. "That's the third time ya phone rang and you looked at it and ain't answer."

"Damn, it's called the iPhone not the Brock phone, nigga. Roll the dice!"

"Aww, you son of a bitch!" he shouted at the four and the three that showed up on the dice after he rolled them.

I picked up the forty dollars off the dash and added it to the knot that was in my pocket. My phone rang again. Brock snatched it off the middle console.

"Give me this mafucka," he said. "I'll answer it." He looked at the screen.

"Stop playin', nigga. Gimme my phone." I didn't want him to answer Leah's call. I really wanted her to get the message that I wasn't fuckin' with her.

"It's Kenny. I see why you duckin' his shady ass."

"I'm not duckin' that nigga. That was some chick the other times."

"So you want me to answer it?"

"Naw. Fuck that nigga, too."

Brock shrugged his shoulders and put my phone back down. "Fuck 'im."

Then he rolled the dice and we went on gambling.

A few minutes later the scanner sounded. *Beeeeep.* "*Medic Nine, Belmont and Montgomery Avenue in the parking area of the Belmont Plateau. Medic Nine, Belmont and Montgomery in the Belmont Plateau parking area. Injuries from an accident.*"

Brock stopped the dice and threw them in his pocket. Then he sat up in the truck, put it in drive, and slammed his foot on the gas. We tore out of the gas station parking lot and headed up Fifty-second street toward Parkside Avenue. From there we hit Fairmount park, took it across Belmont Avenue, and pulled into the parking lot at the Plat. It was pitch-black. No streetlights or nothing.

I could see that there was a dark-colored Denali parked. A few spaces away from it was a green Impala. There was a third car in the distance that looked abandoned. But of all the cars out there, none of them looked like it had been in an accident.

Brock drove up alongside the Denali. It was then that we noticed a group of guys in back of the SUV. Some of them had briefcases and others had Sneaker Villa bags. After a closer look I realized that Kenny was among the group. He started walking toward the truck when he seen us park.

"Fuck is goin' on out here?" I thought aloud.

"Yo," Kenny said when he got to the truck. "You gotta be the most dedicated chaser I know. A hit is called and you come runnin' just like I thought." He smirked.

"You called the hit?" I guessed.

"Yeah, man, you ain't answer my phone call. I needed you to bring the scanners up here and listen out for the law while I took care of this business," Kenny had the nerve to say.

"Nigga, is you retarded?" I asked him, really believing that Kenny had a mental problem. There was no other explanation for his up-and-down behavior. He fucked around and been bipolar. How else could you justify a nigga askin' for help from somebody whose pop he scammed and who the last time he seen him had basically threatened his life. If I had a gun on me I was liable to shoot that nigga where he stood. "You expect me to sit here and be a lookout for you?"

Then Brock chimed in, "If that is the case, that was stupid as hell of you to call a hit up here. By doin' that you just called the cops right to you."

Kenny smiled and said, "I see it took you no time to learn the game. But the cops came and left. I was in the cut watchin' them. Y'all ain't hear them call it unfounded on the scanners? Shit, maybe I don't need y'all niggas up here. Y'all don't pay close attention to the scanners no way." He chuckled.

"Watch out," Brock said to Kenny, opening the truck door.

"Where you goin'?" I asked him.

"Right here," he said. "I gotta piss like a race horse."

"Hurry up, 'cause we out. We ain't sittin' up this mafucka," I said, grillin' Kenny.

Kenny shrugged his shoulders and said, "I called myself burying the hatchet. You woulda got paid well and everything for this one." Then he walked away from the truck and disappeared back behind the Denali with the rest of the group.

I sat up in the passenger's seat, leaned over, and yelled out the driver's window. "Brock, hurry that shit up." I was ready to go. I didn't feel comfortable up there with Kenny and those other niggas whom I didn't know. I felt like a sitting duck.

The sound of the driver's door opening turned my attention to my left, and in a flash I heard a barrage of gunshots.

POP! POP! POP! POP! POP! POP! POP!

"BROOOCCCKK!" I shouted as I witnessed my friend's body jerk back and forth as his torso attracted bullets like metal to magnets.

I went to lean over to pull him in the truck and I felt a strong force hit me in the back of my left shoulder. I put my hand on the spot where I felt the force, and my fingers were instantly drenched in blood.

I thought about climbing over in the driver's seat and peeling out of there, but I didn't want to get hit with another stray. So instead, I ducked down as far as I could.

After a few seconds, I heard the gunfire slow to a stop. Then I heard voices and footsteps right outside my truck.

I slowly sat up in the seat to see who it was and what they were doing.

It was Kenny and his older brother Tim. They were rummaging through the Denali.

"Yo!" Tim called out, pointing to the abandoned car I had noticed when Brock and I first got there. Kenny looked in the direction of the car. "Why the fuck is the horn steady beeping?" Tim asked with frustration.

"His ass got hit, and I bet he's slumped over on the mafucka," Kenny summed up. "I know you got a light, right?"

Tim nodded and pulled a lighter from his pants pocket.

Then Kenny instructed, "Get the gasoline out the trunk and set that mafucka on fire. I'll load the car up, and we out."

Kenny and Tim quickly and methodically performed their tasks— Kenny transportin' briefcases and Sneaker Villa bags from the back of the Denali to the trunk of the Impala, and Tim settin' fire to the car that was in the distance. Meanwhile, I was tryin' to feel around in my truck for my phone to call the cops.

"You was right. That was a mothafuckin' cop!" Tim said, holding up a badge and an ID as he jogged up to Kenny, who was now standing right in front of the truck.

Kenny's face grew perplexed. "Who the fuck was tryna set us up?" He seemed to be thinking aloud.

"Yooo!" I shouted out to get Kenny and his brother's attention. I didn't want to, but I needed to get to a hospital and I couldn't find my phone. So I needed them.

Kenny ran over to the passenger's side and asked, "Nas, you all right?"

"Yeah, but I'm hit!"

"All right. Just chill. Soon as we leave I'll call you an ambulance."

I didn't believe that nigga. I'd rather drive myself to the hospital. I just needed him to help me put Brock in the truck.

"Naw, you ain't gotta call nobody. Just help me get my homie in the truck. I'll drive myself to the hospital."

"Well, then, you might as well go 'head then. Ya homie is dead."

"How you know? Just help me get him in the truck."

"He gone, nigga!"

"All right, even if he is. I ain't leavin' him out here. Help me get him in the truck!"

I got out of the truck and walked around to the driver's side. Brock's lifeless body was facedown on the pavement. I felt like I had to throw up. I was light-headed.

"I can't help you get that nigga in the truck. I'll call y'all an ambulance," he said. "Gimme ya phone."

"It's in the truck somewhere," I said, leaning against the truck. I was feeling weaker.

Kenny hurried over to the passenger's side of the truck and searched around for my phone. He found it and dialed 911. He put it up to my ear and I grabbed it, holding it to my ear with my right hand.

"I been shot," I said in the phone.

Then Kenny mumbled to me, "You came to a call for a tow and got caught in a cross fire. You don't know shit else."

He and Tim then quickly ran to the Impala and got in.

The last thing I saw before I closed my eyes was a blazing fire coming from the car that the cop was in and Kenny and Tim speeding off. And the last thing I heard were my scanners.

Beep . . . "*Medic Nine, Medic Nine, Belmont Avenue and Montgomery Drive, multiple gunshots fired. A male complaintiff shot. Medic Nine, Belmont Avenue and Montgomery Drive, at the Belmont Plateau, multiple shots fired. A male complaintiff wounded.*"

CHASER

Leah

It was four fourteen in the morning when the sound of my security system alerted me that my back door had opened. It woke me out of a good sleep that took me the whole night to get into. I sat up in bed and listened. It was Kenny and, from the sound of it, his brother Tim. What the hell were they doin'? I anticipated that Kenny would have gotten locked up at his meeting. That was supposed to have been the plan. What could have happened that led to Kenny being home and not in jail?

I walked down the hall to the top of the stairs to get a better listen. I heard voices, then the refrigerator door opening and closing, then water starting to run. Next there were footsteps coming upstairs. I decided to go back into my bedroom and pretend to be asleep.

"Leah, wake up! I gotta talk to you," Kenny said the minute he walked in.

I stretched and yawned, then sat up in the bed.

"What's wrong?" I asked, peeking at him as he feverishly washed his hands in our master bathroom.

"Come here," he said, his tone not so pleasant.

I took my time getting up. I was trying to think of all the possible scenarios that could have taken place that morning and what bearings they might have had on me.

I went into the bathroom, stopping at the doorway. "What happened?" I asked, concerned at the sight of blood in the sink.

"Never mind that," Kenny said. "Leah, I need you to tell me everything you and the cop talked about while you was locked up."

I couldn't imagine what had gone wrong during the transaction and what it had to do with me and the cop's discussion while I was in jail. But I knew it couldn't have been anything good. I became unnerved. My heart was in my stomach.

"What do you mean, what we talked about? Pertaining to what?"

Kenny paused from scrubbing his hands and looked at me. "Everything! From beginning to end! I need to know everything!" He said impatiently.

I exhaled and started from the top, hoping the CI training I got before I was released from jail wouldn't fail me. "He basically asked me who put me up to staging the accident. I told him that nobody did and that I wanted to speak to my attorney. He said that I was being charged with three third-degree felonies and was looking at about seven years for each charge. And then he asked if what I did was worth me spending the next twenty years of my life in prison—"

"How did he get on the subject of you becoming an informant?"

I took a hard swallow and said, "He basically asked me if I had any ties to Alliance Collision. I told him I knew the owner's son. He asked if he was the one who put me up to the staging. I told him no. Then he said don't lie to him, and he started telling me that he knew about other things that they had done like this and if I helped them build a case against Alliance, then my case could disappear. I told him I still wanted to speak to an attorney. Then I was put back in my cell and granted bail. That's when I called you to tell you what the bail was, and you told me I should go ahead and give them the information they were lookin' for," I reflected. "Why, what's wrong?"

Kenny dried his hands with a towel, wiped his face off with the same towel, then turned around and leaned his butt against the sink. His hands were folded across his stomach. He was looking straight ahead, focused, as if he was concentrating.

"So when you told him you would do it, did he mention that he had other informants or undercovers watching Nasir and them?"

I thought about my response before giving it. I wasn't trained on how to answer a question as such, so I wanted to be careful. I was already nervous as hell and didn't need any slipups.

I shook my head. "Why? What's wrong? What happened?" I tried to turn the interrogation off me and onto Kenny.

Kenny broke his stare and turned to look at me.

"It was a cop at my meeting spot tonight," Kenny revealed. "And I'm tryin' to put the pieces together to see why he was there and how he could have known about the meeting."

I could feel my heartbeat thumping through my chest. I scanned the room as my mind started focusing on what items were in my reach that I could use as weapons if it came down to it. I was petrified.

"A cop?" I acted as surprised as I possibly could.

"Yeah. And when I first peeped him, we were already in the middle of moving shit, so we couldn't just switch locations. So I asked the bull who I was coppin' from, was he settin' me up? He told me no, so I wanted him to bust shots at the cop's car to prove it to me. He hesitated, so I let a shot off at the car, then somebody else let off shots, and the next thing I know it's a fuckin' shoot-out. Two of my homies got killed, and the niggas I was coppin' from whole squad got plucked off. It was a blood bath out that mafucka . . ." Kenny described.

"Oh my God," I gasped, picturing the sight and drawing the conclusion that Detective Daily was dead. "Tell me you didn't kill a cop."

At that point my knees buckled. I had to grab on to the bathroom door frame to keep myself from falling.

Kenny turned into a drill sergeant. "Get up, Leah! I need you to be strong! The pressure is about to be on, and I'ma need you to be able to withstand it. You hear me?"

"Yes," I muffled, dropping my head.

"Look at me!"

I looked up at him.

"I'ma need you to inform me on *everything* the detective tell you about Nas and them—*everything!* And if you hear about that nigga Nas sayin' my name at all, you need to let me know that shit," Kenny commanded.

I became more confused. "Why would Nasir say your name?"

"Because besides me and Tim, he was the only one that didn't die out there tonight," Kenny explained.

"He was out there?" I asked.

"Yeah," Kenny said. "I had him out there with the scanners to be somewhat of a lookout."

"What?" I couldn't believe what I was hearing. Nasir too mad at me to take any of my calls, but he would agree to be a lookout for Kenny, who had just as much fault as me in using his dad's accounts to wash money.

"I know." Kenny shook his head. "That was stupid as shit of me, knowin' the nigga's pop and they whole business is under investigation. But that shit didn't even dawn on me at the time. But anyway, I know the cops goin' be houndin' him for information. And being as though he got hit and his homie got killed, he might be prone to give it to 'em."

I was floored taking in all the information Kenny was giving me. First, Detective Daily was dead, then Nasir was hit, and his homie, whom I presumed to be Brock, was killed. I didn't have time to deal with one issue before he had hit me with another and another.

"So I'ma need you to be my eyes and ears while you workin' with the cops. In the meantime, I need to get to the bottom of why the cop was out there in the first place. I need to find out who is hippin' the mafuckin' law to my shit."

Kenny stood up straight and rubbed his palm over his low haircut. He brushed past me as he left out the bathroom. Then he came back.

"Oh, and everything that we talk about stays between you and me! You understand?"

"Yes," I whimpered, my eyes staring down at the floor.

"Look at me," he said.

I turned around and raised my head. Tears streaming down my face, I looked at him.

Then, in a cold and calculated tone, he said, "I don't have no problems knockin' anybody off if I even think they takin' shots at my freedom, you dig?"

I managed to nod, even though my body had stiffened up. My lungs felt like they were closing, and I found myself unable to breathe.

"That goes for you and anybody the fuck else," he added. Then he left again.

I collapsed to the floor, panting. I was scared breathless.

Nasir

It was the Tuesday after Memorial Day, and I was laid up in the hospital recovering from a bullet wound that had shattered my collarbone. Much worse, though, I was mourning the loss of my best friend. I couldn't believe Brock was gone. Not Brock, of all people. That was one nigga who never did shit to nobody. He stayed outta trouble, stayed out the way. And all he ever wanted to do was have fun. It hurt like hell picturing his body stretched out on the pavement with all those bullet holes through it, and I'd found myself shedding more tears in the last forty-eight hours than I had in my entire life.

"I'm sorry. I'm so sorry," I repeatedly apologized to the nurse for having to clean vomit off me again.

"It's okay, Mr. Freeman. It's not your fault. You don't have to be so apologetic," she said as she wiped me clean.

"I know. But it's embarrassin' to keep spittin' up on myself."

"You can't control it. You're just one of those patients who can't take morphine. Consider that a good thing."

The room grew silent as the nurse continued cleaning me up. She threw the sponge in the bucket that was by my bed and rinsed it. She had a smile on her face the whole time and tried to make me feel okay, but I felt fucked up. I was a grown man throwin' up on himself and I couldn't even clean it off. The only thing that kept me sane was the fact that I was alive. I could've easily been another homicide victim.

"Oh, it looks like you have visitors," the nurse said as she helped changed my gown. She gathered her cleaning items and started out the room.

I looked toward the door. Once I got past the bouquet of "Get Well" balloons I realized it was my mom and my dad.

My mom was smiling and crying at the same time as she walked over to my bed. Leaning over, she kissed me on my forehead. I hugged her with my right arm, the one that wasn't in a sling.

"Stop crying," I told her.

She unwrapped the balloon strings from around her hand and let the balloons coast to the ceiling. Meanwhile, my dad shook his head as he greeted me with a handshake.

"How you feelin', man?" he asked, as if it pained him to talk to me.

"Aww, man, I'm alive. That's all that matters," I responded, holding back.

"Thank God," my mom chimed in, shaking her head. "Thank God." My mom wiped tears from her eyes and then blew her nose. Her legs were shaking uncontrollably. She was an emotional wreck. She couldn't get herself together.

"Mom, calm down," I said. "It's just a broken bone. It'll heal."

"You don't understand," she said. "You my firstborn, and just the thought of losing you is driving me crazy. And like I told ya dad last night, we should never go a day without tellin' our kids we love them. Let alone go weeks without even speakin' to them." My mom's tears returned. "He would have had a heart attack if you would've been taken from us, especially while y'all were goin' through y'all shit. If y'all don't do nothin' else, y'all need to squash the bullshit."

Then my dad cut in. "It's squashed. This my son. That little shit that happened can't change that."

I nodded to my mom to assure her that I was willing to squash the beef as well. "Life is too short to be holdin' on to grudges," I said.

"I just wanna get to the bottom of what happened and who did this shit," my dad said, switching the subject. "The cops said you told them you went up there for a tow and shots rang out."

"Yeah, pretty much." I stuck to my story. I didn't want to tell anybody that Kenny had something to do with the shooting because I wanted to handle him on my own.

"So you didn't see the pussies?"

I shook my head.

"Not one of them? 'Cause I'm convinced this wasn't no fuckin' accident. They hit Brock up like they wanted to kill that nigga, and lookin' at the truck, I'm lucky to still have my son," my dad expressed.

"Soon as I heard the shots I ducked down, and that's why I couldn't see nothin'."

My dad rubbed his goatee and asked, "What were you doin' a tow for at one in the morning anyway? Matter of fact, what were you doin' a tow for, period?" My dad knew better. He knew that I didn't tow cars unless they were hits I had gotten.

"Normally I wouldn't have took the call. But Brock ain't never do a tow before, and since he was chasin' full-time now, I told him he needed to learn. So I figured that would be a good time to show him how to hook a car. Plus, it had been slow all night, a bunch of domestic disputes," I recalled. "I ain't think it would hurt us to leave the post for a minute and do a quick tow." I came up with a good excuse. I usually kept it 100 percent with my dad about stuff like that, but I knew the minute I mentioned Kenny's name he would be out huntin' that nigga down. And that was my battle—one I wanted to fight.

"Let me ask you somethin'," my dad said.

"What's that?"

"What else are you doin' besides chasin'?" he asked.

"Nothin'. I mean, I run my bodily injury cases, too, but that's it."

"Seriously, Nas, you can tell me," he said. "Are you hustlin'?"

I smirked and said, "No!"

"Honestly," my dad insisted, looking me in the eyes.

"Naw, I'm keepin' it one hundred. I don't sell drugs."

My dad took a deep breath and nodded. "All right," he said, sounding only halfway convinced. "If that's ya story and you stickin' to it, cool. But it ain't addin' up to me, Nas. I mean, somebody set you and Brock the fuck up! And if that's the case, let this be a lesson to you. Watch the company you keep. And don't let me find out you protectin' the nigga who did this, 'cause you don't want me to get at 'im! 'Cause I'm ya father, and that's a decision for me to make not for you to make for me!"

My mom cut in, "Let's not talk about all of that, please."

"I'm just sayin'," my dad continued, "I was chasin' for six years before I opened the shop. And when I was scratchin' and scrapin' on the streets, everybody was cool with me. But soon as I opened the shop and started making real money, that's when I started seeing niggas for who they really were. The same niggas who I called my friends started turnin' against me. They couldn't stand the fact that I was makin' so much more money than them, and some of them were actually hustlin', puttin' their lives on the line, riskin' their freedom and still comin' in second to a nigga like me who was on the straight and narrow. Niggas hate to see a nigga doin' good, let alone doin' better than themselves. Like that nigga Kenny. He don't keep you close 'cause y'all was best friends. He keep you close because misery loves company and success breeds envy, son."

My dad was sharp. He knew in his gut that Kenny had somethin' to do with my bein' shot and Brock gettin' killed. He just wanted me to come out and say it. But I didn't want to.

My dad concluded his father-to-son by saying that he was goin' to find out who shot me. He was goin' to put the word out in the streets that he was lookin' for whoever did, and when it got back to him, he was goin' take care of the nigga. I believed my dad, too. He was older and settled, yes, but he had the kind of past that could never completely desert him. He was from the streets and had no problem returning to them if need be.

For the remainder of their visit, my mom and dad went on to discuss other things, like when the doctors planned on discharging me and how long it was going to take for my broken collarbone to heal. After about an hour and a half they left. Before they did, though, my dad demanded that I give him any and all information about the shooting as it came to me. I gave him my word that I would.

Leah

The holiday had passed, and the country got back to work. That meant Kenny, too. This was the first day since the mayhem that broke out during Memorial Day weekend that he had left the house. I took his absence as an opportunity to take care of some personal business.

I was standing in the parking lot of the doctor's office with a lot on my mind. My fears were confirmed. I was pregnant. I didn't know by whom, though. After calculating the time between the last time I had sex with either Kenny or Nasir and when I had my last period, I concluded that Nasir was likely the father. But, of course, I wasn't absolutely sure. And I didn't want to point fingers without being able to prove anything. I didn't want to embarrass myself. It was bad enough I was in such a situation. I had never been that type of girl.

I decided against telling anybody. I didn't know what I was going to do just yet, whether or not I was going to keep it or get an abortion. So I decided I would keep the news to myself for now.

The next thing I wanted to do with my free time was go to the hospital to see Nasir in person. Regardless how he felt about me, I still had love for him and wanted to make sure he was all right.

I drove to the University of Pennsylvania on Thirty-fourth and Spruce and parked in visitor's parking. I found out Nasir's room number, and before I went up to the Trauma and Critical Care Unit, I stopped at the gift shop and bought Nasir a get-well gift.

When I got to his floor, I was stopped at the nurse's station and asked who I was there to see. I gave Nasir's name. They called his room and asked if it was okay for me to come in. I stood there, anxious, hoping Nasir wouldn't refuse me.

I desperately wanted to see him and console him. I wanted him to know that I really loved him and that I was sorry about what had happened to him and Brock. I also wanted to get his side of the story about what had happened at the shoot-out. I needed some information to take with me to the police station when I went later that afternoon. Not only did Kenny jeopardize the deal I had with the detective by killing him, his constant bullshit made it more and more of a strain to live with him. He needed to be locked up.

Nasir

I was alone again with time to think. But not for long. I got a call from the nurse's station alerting me that I had a visitor by the name of Leah Baker. I was reluctant about accepting her visit, but I ended up telling the nurse it was all right for her to come in. I was curious to see what she was going to say and how she was going to feel.

Leah walked in my hospital room slowly and hesitantly. She had a small basket of flowers in her hands, which she extended to me as she approached my bedside.

"Oh my God, Nasir, look at you," she sang, one hand over her mouth, sorrow in her eyes.

I sat up in bed to accept the basket. I read the tag: Get Well Soon.

I put the flowers on the tray table. Then I lay back in my bed.

"Good lookin'," I said, dispassionate.

"Of course," she responded. "It's the least I could do." Then she broke out in tears and blurted out, "Nasir, I'm so sorry!"

I rolled my eyes and asked, "When aren't you sorry, Leah? It seem like I'm constantly travelin' down this same road with you. Like every time I turn around I'm caught up in some serious drama 'cause of you or ya boy. I'm through with it. I learned. So don't worry about apologizin' to me. Just accept the fact that I don't wanna be a part of ya life anymore and move on." I sighed, having gotten my feelings off my chest.

Leah's face dimmed with pity. She shook her head as she stood over my bed. Leaning over, she wrapped her arms around me, hugging me. "You don't mean that," she said.

"Yes, I do," I maintained. "Now, if you don't mind, I'd like it if you'd leave so I can get through the rest of the day on a happier note."

Leah withdrew her arms from around me. "Okay, I deserve that," she said, seemingly gathering her composure. "I'll leave, but before I do, I just want to get your side of the story about what happened Saturday night, Sunday morning."

Before I could say anything or ask what she cared for, like I wanted to, I got a call from the nurse's station saying that I had a visitor who said his name was Kenny.

Fuck this nigga want, I thought. "You can send him in," I said. I hung the phone up and told Leah, "Ya man 'bout to come in here." Still, I was nonchalant.

"Oh my God! Are you for real? What am I goin' to do? I can't leave. He'll see me in the hallway." She panicked, just like I had thought she would.

"It amazes me how you keep comin' at me askin' me to forgive you and to take you back, but every time you seem to have this undying love for Kenny. I mean, what you care that he's on his way in here for if you love me like you say you do?"

"Nasir, for the last time, that is not the case," Leah pleaded. Then, looking around in panic, Leah scampered to the bathroom and closed the door.

Seconds later in walked Kenny.

"What's up, cannon?" He greeted me with a smile on his face, as if there was something to celebrate.

"Whatchu doin' here, man?" I asked him, a frown on my face to let him know exactly how I felt. "You got some nerve comin' up here."

"Daaamn," he said. "I just came up here to see how you was makin' out and shit. Give my condolences, that's all."

I went to say something but was distracted by Kenny's sudden change of focus. I followed his eyes as they locked in on something that was in my bed. They landed on a Dior key chain that was peeping out from underneath the white blanket. It must've been Leah's. She must've have dropped it when she gave me a hug. I started to make up a lie about the key chain and say something like my mom left it by accident, but I changed my mind. I didn't care anymore about trying to hide the fact that Leah and I had had something in the past. I was done giving a fuck about Kenny and how he felt.

Kenny stepped back and looked at me like he was confused.

I looked back at him as if to say, What, nigga?

Then he put his hand on his chin and started reminiscing. "Remember back when we was chasin' together? You called yaself beatin' me to a hit and hauled ass through that stop sign—"

I cut Kenny off. With my teeth clenched and my eyes squinted, I warned, "Don't fuckin' do it, man! Don't fuckin' do it!"

Kenny chuckled. "Do what?"

"Throw that shit in my mafuckin' face! That shit stops today! You hear me? I been paid you back for that shit! Up until two days ago, nigga, I been payin' you back for that shit! I got shot *and* my man lost his life in the process! And you come up in this mafucka like I still owe you?"

Kenny's anger matched mine and he shouted, "I DIDN'T HIT THAT OLD LADY! YOU DID! BUT BECAUSE I AIN'T SAY SHIT, THAT SHIT ATE AWAY AT MY MOTHAFUCKIN' CON-SCIENCE!"

"AWW, NIGGA, WHO THE FUCK YOU THINK YOU PLAYIN'? YOU AIN'T GOT NO MAFUCKIN' CONSCIENCE! NOT THEN AND NOT THE FUCK NOW!"

"AND APPARENTLY YOU AIN'T GOT ONE, EITHER, NIGGA! THAT'S WHY YOU THINK IT'S COOL TO FUCK MY GIRL?"

With my head up I looked Kenny in his eyes and said quietly, "My conscience ain't lead me in that direction. My dick did!" I hit him where it hurt.

In that instant Kenny pulled a four-five out of his waistband, grabbed me by my neck, and shoved the gun in my mouth. It felt like a couple of my teeth had been knocked loose.

"You lucky you worth more to me alive!" Kenny said, then he re-moved the gun from my mouth.

I spit blood out in Kenny's direction. "YOU SHOULDA KILLED ME, NIGGA!"

"If I wanted you dead, I woulda killed you when I killed ya boy, Brock."

I jumped out the bed and lunged at Kenny with my one good arm. He blocked my swing. Then he put me in a headlock, causing me excruciating pain.

"Fuck you surprised for? You didn't think I was goin' leave wit-nesses, did you? The only reason why I left you alive was 'cause Leah ain't done gettin' information out ya ass. You ain't think she was fuckin'

you 'cause you got that curly-ass hair, did you? Naw, she was fuckin'
you to get tape about all the crooked shit you and ya pop be doin'.
Why you think she started workin' at the shop? She ain't need that
measly paper, dog. She agreed to be an informant to get us out that
fraud case we caught."

Kenny let me go and I fell against the hospital bed. The pain in my
shoulder was too great for me to retaliate. All I could do was listen to
the shit he was tellin' me and die inside.

He straightened up his clothes and headed out of my room. Then
he stopped and said, "I know she around this mothafucka somewhere!
Tell her I said job well done!" Then he walked out the room, slamming the door closed behind him.

I heard the bathroom door open slowly. Then Leah's frightened
face peeped around the corner. She was crying.

I didn't care though. I wanted to smash her head in the wall immediately. If only I could.

"What the fuck did you drag me into?" I snapped, tears coming to
my eyes. I was so mad I could feel the veins popping out my neck just
from looking at Leah. "You tryna set me and my family up? So all this
time you was just usin' me for information?"

Leah shook her head repeatedly as she tried to get a word in.

"I wanna fuck you up, Leah! You played me, dog? That's why you
was launderin' that money through my pop? So you could catch him
up on that shit, too? YOU AIN'T SHIT!"

Leah finally was able to speak, "NASIR! LISTEN TO ME!
KENNY DON'T KNOW WHAT HE'S TALKIN' ABOUT! HE'S
JUST TRYIN' TO GET BACK AT YOU FOR MESSIN' WITH
ME! IT'S HIM I'M GETTIN' TAPE ON, LIKE I TRIED TO
TELL YOU BEFORE!"

"That's what you'll have me believe! But if it was that, why the
fuck you just ask me to give you my side of the story about what happened the other night? Huh? Huh? Answer me that! That was proba-

bly ya only motive for comin' up this mafucka! To get info! You wasn't comin' up here to see me!" I reached over and grabbed the flowers off the tray table and threw them at her.

She ducked and screamed. Then the begging began. "Nasir, please! If ever there was a time that I needed you to trust me, now is it!" she cried.

"Fuck you, Leah!" I said sternly, throwing her keys to her as hard as I could. "Get the fuck out!"

Leah picked up her keys and asked if I could hear her out one last time.

I shook my head and told her, "You dead to me, man!"

She stood still for a minute, sobbing. A look of despair covered her face. Then she turned to the door and walked out.

I managed to pull myself onto the bed. Trying to ignore the pain I was in, I felt around on my bed for my cell phone. When I found it, I dialed my dad. I realized that with my injury I wouldn't be able to get at Kenny the way I wanted so badly to. I didn't just want to shoot the nigga and kill 'im. I wanted to torture that slimy mafucka! And for that, I needed my dad's assistance.

"What's up, Nas?" my dad answered.

"Dad, I got some information on who did it."

"I'll rap to you about it when you get home."

"All right."

"It's goin' get handled."

"All right."

"I love you, son."

"I love you, too, Dad.

CHASER

Leah

left the hospital after seeing Nasir and went straight to the police station, ready either to accept my charges or to tell the cops everything Kenny had told me about what had gone down at the shootout and hope that it would lead to his arrest. Whatever needed to be done to get Kenny out my life I was goin' do. If not, I was goin' end up dead. Either Kenny was goin' kill me for fuckin' with Nasir, or he was goin' drive me to kill myself.

I went inside the precinct and told the clerk why I was there. She immediately led me to an interview room in the back. I waited anxiously for somebody to come in and tell me what had happened to Detective Daily.

After a few minutes, the door opened. I picked my face up out my palms and looked up.

"Detective Daily?" I was shocked to see that he was alive.

"Leah, why did you come in? Why didn't you call me first? It isn't a good idea for you to be seen walkin' in and out of here."

"I had to. I thought somethin' happened to you at the last location," I told him.

"No, I didn't go that night. I was down at the shore for the holiday." The detective's eyes grew weary. "It was my partner who was killed."

"I'm sorry to hear that, Detective. I didn't know that it was goin' to come to that. I just thought he was goin' make the transaction and that be that. I never would've put you or anybody in harm's way," I cried, unable to control my emotions.

"I know, kiddo," he said. "You couldn't have known. Neither could I. But we can't dwell on that. Right now we have to move swiftly to get the perpetrator. Tell me you got something on that son of a bitch." He got straight to it.

I nodded eagerly. "He killed your partner."

"How are you sure of this?" Detective Daily asked just eagerly.

"He told me that once he realized there was a cop out there, he let a shot off."

The detective was taking notes in a pad. He stopped and started snapping his fingers at somebody who was apparently watching us from the outside. "Was there anybody with him that you know of?"

"His brother was."

"And what's his name?"

"Timothy Courtland."

"And do you know his address?"

I gave the detective Tim's address.

Another detective entered the interview room, and Detective Daily turned his attention to him. "We've got our perp," he told the other detective.

"Who is it and where can we find him?"

"Kenneth Courtland. 210 Morton Road."

"We'll go pick 'im up now."

"Get his brother, too." Detective Daily stood up and handed the other detective the piece of paper he had been writing on, which he ripped from his notepad. "Timothy Courtland. 5412 Gainor Road. In case Kenneth doesn't budge. We'll try to get his brother to give 'im up. Either way, we need both of these men in custody. We need to get a confession out of one or the other so we can charge them both with murder one. Put out an alert and take caution, 'cause they're likely to be armed and dangerous," Detective Daily passed down the chain of command.

Then he sat back down and patted my knee. "You're gonna be all right, kiddo. We're gonna nab this bastard."

"Please do, Detective. Because it's at the point where I'm scared for my life."

"Has he threatened you? Does he know that you're working with us?"

"No, no. But he knows somebody tipped y'all. And he's on a rampage, and I don't wanna cross paths with him. I don't even wanna go home until y'all bring him in."

"That's no problem, Ms. Baker. We will arrange for you to stay in a hotel until we get him."

Detective Daily put me up in the Comfort Inn all the way in South Philly on Delaware Avenue. I was sitting in the hotel room all alone, scared and confused. I thought about where I was in my life and started pitying myself. How had I let things come to this? Before Kenny, I was a student and I'd worked two jobs. I had a social life. I had friends. I had a good relationship with my mom. Now I didn't have any of that. It was like my life took a 360-degree turn for the worst when I got with Kenny. And I was tired of accepting it. I wanted to sever all ties with him and start fresh. I had even decided to abort the baby I had recently found out I was carrying. Just in case it was his.

I felt guilty for thinking that way about a baby—about my baby—but I didn't know what else to think.

I got in the shower and ordered food, hoping it would relax me a little. Then while I was waiting for my food to come I got a phone call. It was from Kenny. I didn't answer right away. I had to get my story together first.

"Hello," I answered after the fourth ring.

"Where the hell you at?" Kenny asked.

I began to whisper, "I'm in hiding, Kenny" I told him. "The police found out that somebody tipped Vic and Nasir off about me being an informant and they immediately put me in protective custody."

"Wasn't you at the hospital today *with* Nasir?"

I couldn't lie. He knew I was there. If I had lied about that, nothing else I would have said would have been credible. "Yeah. How you know?" I played it off.

"I was up there. I saw ya fuckin' key chain. What's goin' on, Leah? And don't tell me no bullshit, either! 'Cause this nigga told me y'all fuckin'! And he lucky I didn't knock his ass off right there in the ma-fuckin' hospital!"

"Kenny, Kenny, listen to me," I sniveled. "I would never cross no lines like that. You gotta trust me. The only reason why I've been dealin' with Nasir in the first place was to get us out the shit we were in. You *know* that. I'm not doin' nothin' with Nasir, and I never did! If he told you that, he lied! I don't know what for, maybe to get under your skin, but that shit ain't true! I went to the hospital today, yes, but only because the cops wanted me to go up there and try to get information out of Nasir about who shot that cop," I tried to convince him. "When I couldn't get anything out of him, I left and went straight to the police station. My key chain must've fell off my keys," I explained, with as much sincerity in my tone as I could muster.

Kenny was quiet for a minute. Then he said, "Loyalty is everything to me, Leah, and if for one second I feel like I'm not gettin' it from you, you know what can happen, don't you?"

"I know. And my loyalty to you is the one thing you don't have to question," I assured him.

"Well, good. 'Cause I need you right now more than anytime before."

"What's goin' on?"

"I think Nasir mentioned my name to the cops. They been showin' up at everybody house lookin' for me."

"Where are you? What are you goin' to do?"

"I'm in the cut. But I'm tryna plan shit out now. Run this by me again. The cops got word that Nasir knows you was snitchin', so they got you hidin' out?"

"Yeah. Pretty much. And I'm scared, Kenny," I tried hard to convey weakness. "I'm scared for you, and I'm scared for me."

"Don't be scared. I'ma see that nigga before he see any one of us. If he's out the equation, then you'll be cool and there won't be nobody to point the finger at me in the courtroom talkin' about I killed that cop. When I think about it, I shouldn't have left him alive from the gate."

"Kenny, I don't want you bein' stupid. Now, I know we're in a tight spot right now, but you can't lose yourself. You can't just go up in the hospital and think you can do somethin' to Nasir without bein' caught."

"I ain't goin' do that. I ain't gotta do that. I know where he be. Matter of fact, I know he goin' go to Brock's funeral. I know that much."

At that, I was eager to get off the phone with Kenny. I wanted to let Detective Daily know where he could possibly catch up with Kenny.

I dialed the number. "Detective, I just talked to Kenny," I said without delay.

"Did he give you any information about his whereabouts?"

"No. But he did say he planned to go to one of the guys who was killed funeral."

"Which guy, Ms. Baker?"

"Brakir Jackson. Everybody called him Brock."

"We'll have to pick 'im up there then. Thanks for this."

"Just make sure y'all get him fast because how he was talkin' he plans to do somethin' to Nasir. He thinks Nasir ratted him out, and that's why y'all are lookin' for him."

"Okay. Thanks for this. And soon as we get him into custody, we will let you know."

I got off the phone and felt drained. My situation was getting more and more complicated by the hour. I was in a whirlwind of drama, and I didn't know how I was going to get out. All I knew was that I wanted out. I wanted out desperately.

Nasir

A day out of the hospital I was preparing to go Brock's funeral. I was putting on my clothes slowly, partly because it was hard trying to dress myself with one arm in a sling, but partly because I wasn't in a hurry to go bury my friend.

"The trucks are here," my mom yelled up to me.

I was at my mom's house. I came straight here from the hospital yesterday and spent the night. While I was in the hospital my mom had gone to my apartment and grabbed some clothes and personal items for me. I planned on staying with her and my dad until I healed some.

I looked out the window of my old bedroom. It was like a parade outside. Two limousines led a line of about two dozen tow trucks, the first truck being a flatbed with my old truck on top of it. Spray painted on the windows was *R.I.P. BROCK 1983–2008*. And on the hood was an airbrushed picture of Brock.

"You all right?" my mom asked, as I walked down the steps.

"I'm cool," I said, the depressed tone in my voice not matching my response.

My dad and my two younger brothers, who I wasn't too close with due to our ten- and twelve-year age differences, came walking downstairs minutes after me.

"Yo, is that real?" my thirteen-year-old brother asked me, grabbing my wrist and examining my all-diamond Cartier.

"Yeah, dummy. Tell 'im, Nas. He don't know nothin' about ice," my fifteen-year-old brother answered for me.

I chuckled at the two of them. They reminded me of myself when I was younger.

"Y'all go get in the limo," my mom instructed.

They did what they were told, and then my dad and I followed suit. We pulled up to Brock's mom's house, and damn near the whole block was outside waiting to follow us to the funeral. Brock's mom, grandmom, and sister got in the limo with us while some of Brock's other relatives got in the second limo. Friends, neighbors, and distant relatives got in their cars and lined up behind the trucks. We all made our way to Calvary Baptist Church on Haverford Avenue, where Brock's mom was a member.

The church was already packed before we got there. So when all of us got inside, it was overcrowded. A lot of Brock's friends from his neighborhood were there. They all had on T-shirts with the same picture of Brock that was on the hood of the tow truck. I even noticed a lot of police officers present.

The family lined up in pairs to view the body before taking our seats. The hardest part for me was hearing Brock's mom grieve. The cries that came from that lady expressed a pain no mother should have to bare. I thought about my own mom and prayed silently that she would never have to lay any one of her sons to rest. I wished I could guarantee it, too, but the reality was we lived in a city during a time where death by gun violence was at an all-time high. And it didn't even matter if you were doin' dirt or not. You could get hit with a stray or be killed during a robbery or home invasion. It was that crazy in Philly. Niggas was shootin' any and everything, in broad daylight, at playgrounds, outside of schools. It didn't matter.

After the hour-long funeral service, we all gathered to go to the cemetery. My dad was one of the six pallbearers who had taken the coffin from the church to the hearse. Because of my injury, I couldn't help, even though I wanted to.

At the cemetery the preacher said a few words, prayed, and then allowed for family members and friends to lay a rose on top of the coffin before it was lowered into the ground. It was then that I noticed Kenny. He walked up to the front, laid his rose, and glanced up at me. He had a smirk on his face. I watched him like a hawk while he parted back through the crowd to take his standing position on the outside of the huddle.

I was furious. I wanted to fuck Kenny up. How dare he come to Brock's funeral? I didn't want to make a scene at the burial, but I needed to get some shit off my chest. I needed to confront Kenny. I took a few steps headed in the direction of where Kenny was standing. But my dad came behind me, grabbing my arm.

"Don't do it," he whispered to me. "Not here, not now. Next thing you know, the cops'll think you were a coconspirator."

"What cops?" I asked, mad enough not to care.

My dad nodded his head as a gesture for me to look in Kenny's direction. And walking up on Kenny were two plainclothes cops. They flashed their badges to Kenny and then escorted him to a silver Ford Taurus.

The distraction caused Brock's mom, to stand up and start yelling, "IS THAT THE BASTARD WHO KILLED MY SON? I KNOW

HE DIDN'T HAVE THE AUDACITY TO SHOW UP HERE! IS THAT THE SON OF A BITCH WHO TOOK MY ONLY SON FROM ME? FOR CHRIST SAKE, THAT BETTER NOT BE!"

The preacher and others tried calming Brock's mom, who couldn't stop yelling and sobbing.

Meanwhile, Kenny shot me a nasty look through the rear window as the unmarked police car was being driven away from the burial.

I guessed it was obvious how pissed off I was, because my dad volunteered, "Don't worry. We goin' see that nigga. We goin' get at 'im when he least expect it. Him and his rotten bitch. I knew she was trouble from the beginning. I should've followed my instincts and never hired her ass. 'Cause now I'ma have to kill 'er."

Leah

I stayed two nights in the hotel and then was able to go home. And not because Kenny was being detained, either, because the detectives had to wound up letting him go. When they arrested him, he surprisingly didn't have a weapon on him. When they got a warrant to search our house, they found nothing. They tried for sixteen hours to get him or his brother Tim to talk, and neither of them did. Eventually, the cops had to let them go. They didn't have any evidence to charge them with anything, and they explained to me that they couldn't keep them without bringing charges up against them.

I was getting frustrated with the system and the cops' inability to use the information I had been giving them. I was beginning to feel like I made a mistake by ever agreeing to be an informant in the first place. It seemed like it wasn't worth the trouble or the risks. I wanted to call it quits, but the detectives convinced me that I had come too far to stop now. They told me that they were extremely close to making an arrest, especially while Kenny was scared. They said criminals usually slipped up when they were under pressure.

So the last tactic they wanted to employ was something I was very worried about. I mean, it was already frightening enough to be a snitch, but Detective Daily wanted me to wear a wire and try to get a confession out of Kenny. I refused at first, because the danger in being wired was too grave. But after the detectives explained to me that Kenny was a flight risk and that if I didn't help them get him within the net couple days, he would most likely flee and take me with him. I cringed at the thought of being on the run with Kenny and gave in to the detectives. I'd rather risk my life trying to turn Kenny in than be on the run with him.

The detectives spent a great deal of time coaching me through what I was to say, do, and how I was to act when I got home. They had me wear a covert body wire that would be almost impossible to detect. And considering the fact that Kenny would be busy trying to plan an escape, they felt I would be safe wearing it.

When I walked in my house, it looked like a tornado had hit it. The police ransacked it. Shit was broken, tossed around, and turned upside down.

"What the hell happened in here?" I asked, as if I didn't know the minute I walked in the door.

I crept through the living room, kitchen, family room, and dining room, and when I didn't see Kenny, I went upstairs. I got to our bedroom, and the door was closed. I opened it slowly and was greeted by the barrel of gun.

I was so scared I couldn't scream. I just froze up.

"Shit, Leah!" Kenny gasped. "You almost got ya ass shot! Why you ain't announce yaself?"

I exhaled and put my hand to my heart. "I didn't know anyone was here."

Kenny put his gun back in its holster in the front of his pants. Then he got back to what he obviously was doing before I got there— packing clothes.

"The mafuckas came and snatched me up from the funeral yesterday afternoon. They had me at the police station for damn near twenty-four hours tryin' to break me. And while I was in there, they got a warrant and tore the house up. Good thing I ain't have shit in here," Kenny explained, rushing his words to match the speed of his actions.

I was still startled from having a gun in my face, so I couldn't focus on everything I was told to say and do by the detectives. I found myself just acting off my emotions.

"So what are you goin' to do now?"

"I'm gettin' the fuck outta here. My brother on his way here with a rental."

"Why are you runnin'?"

Kenny stopped what he was doing and looked up at me. "What you mean, why am I runnin'? The cops is on my ass, that's why!"

"But they don't have shit on you!"

"As long as Nasir got breath in his body, the cops got somethin' on me. And I can't get at the nigga just yet."

"Okay, so they got a witness. But it's ya word against his. They can't prove you did anything if you didn't."

"Yeah, but that's just it, Leah. I did do somethin'. That's why the fuck I'm gettin' outta here."

I sat down on the bed next to the suitcase that Kenny was throwin' clothes into. Being close to him was mandatory in order to get his words clear on tape, the detectives had told me. But it was also a death trap, if you asked me. I was sweating profusely, and I hoped Kenny took it as my being scared for him as opposed to my being up to something.

"Yeah, well, they would have to prove it, and they obviously can't if they let you go after interrogatin' you for sixteen hours. But if you run, that's half the proof right there."

"And if I don't run and they find my gun and run it through ballistics and see that the bullets match the one that killed that sucker-ass cop, and then they dust it and my fingerprints come up and they get a statement from Nas, then they got their proof and they got me."

I shook my head. "I don't understand. Why won't you just get rid of the gun?"

"If I could I would, Leah. After I shot that fuckin' cop, shit got chaotic. I was movin' too fast. I thought I threw the gun in the trunk of the Impala, but when we dumped the car I didn't see it in there. I don't know if I dropped it or what. But I ain't waitin' around to see."

I felt butterflies in my stomach. Kenny had just given me the confession the detectives needed. I tried to remain collected, though. It wasn't over yet.

"Leah, look at me," Kenny said. "The cops ain't say nothin' to you about me, did they? Are they askin' questions about me or my brother?"

I bent my eyebrows and shook my head. I felt so much tension between us.

"You know I would fuckin' kill you if you ever snitched on me? You know that, right?"

Ignoring the unimaginable fear I felt in my heart, I tried hard to display loyalty. "Kenny, I would kill myself."

Kenny looked me in my eyes for some seconds before reacting to my comment. Then he smirked and proceeded to tell me his plan.

"I'm goin' lay low in a hotel until Monday. I need you to meet up

CHASER

with Sammy and get my bread. He goin' have it all ready for you. Then you goin' meet up with Dahwoo and he goin' bring it to me. After you finish the shit you doin' with the cops, you can call me and come to where I'm at. But I ain't goin' be able to bring you with me while you got ties to the law. I'll get caught."

"Okay," I complied. Anything to get Kenny to leave so that the cops could arrest him the minute he turned the corner.

Kenny's phone rang as he zipped up his suitcase.

"You outside?"

"I'm comin' now."

Kenny leaned down and kissed me on my lips. "I appreciate you ridin' for me, Leah." Then he left the bedroom.

When the alarm system alerted me that the back door had been opened, confirming Kenny's departure, I didn't hesitate callin' Detective Daily.

"Did y'all get that?"

"We did. We're tailin' the car now. It's almost over, kiddo,"

At that, I hung up with the detective and started packing a bag for myself. Freedom felt near, and I was itchin' to get at it. I didn't even care to leave the bulk of my things behind. I just needed a few necessities and some clothes to last me a couple of weeks.

I sent a text to Nasir just to clear things up with him once and for all. Then I called my mom to let her know that I was on my way over there.

I grabbed my overnight bag and headed out of my bedroom. When I got to the stairs, Kenny appeared out of nowhere.

"How did you know I was in interrogation for sixteen hours?" he asked.

I had a boatload of questions at that point: What was Kenny still doin' there? Who were the detectives tailin' if it wasn't Kenny? Had he heard my call to Detective Daily? But even though I felt like I was caught, I couldn't unmask the truth prematurely. When I first agreed to be an informant against Kenny, I decided I was goin' to ride it all the way out to the end. And that's what I had to do.

"You told me," I responded.

"I said I was in there for damn near twenty-four hours," Kenny refreshed my memory. "How did you know it was exactly sixteen?"

I didn't say anything, and my silence prompted Kenny to grip me by my neck. He pushed me against the wall, held his gun to my temple with one hand, and searched me with the other. When he came across the wire, he snatched it off me. My mind went blank as I tried to think up an excuse. And before any words could slip off my tongue, Kenny's balled fist struck my face with so much force, it felt like I was hit with a brick. I instantly blacked out.

CHASER

Nasir

It was the day after Brock's funeral. I had went home to get some more of my clothes. When I got back to my mom and dad's house, I noticed several unfamiliar cars in the driveway. I parked my car and walked up to the door. I let myself in with the key I'd had ever since I'd lived there. I walked straight back to the kitchen. My mom was sitting in the breakfast nook drinking a glass of wine. My grandmom was sitting opposite her.

"Nasir," my mom said at the sight of me. She stood up to hug me. Then my grandmom did the same.

"What's up, Mom? What's up, Grandmom? Where's dad at?"

"All the men are out back," my grandmom said.

"What's wrong?" I asked, noticin' tears in my mom's puffy eyes.

My mom broke down. "Nasir, what is goin' on? What are y'all gettin' y'allselves into? Ya dad won't tell me anything. But he called ya uncles over here and some other guys, and whenever they're around, trouble is right behind them. I don't know what y'all are plannin' to do, but I hope it's nothin' crazy. I came this close to losin' you." My mom held up her pointer finger over her thumb to indicate a pinch. "And I don't wanna ever have to walk down that road again," she cried.

"And God willing, you won't ever have to walk down that road again." I tried to comfort her. "You just trippin', that's all, Mom. Ain't nothin' goin' happen to nobody."

"I don't know about that, Nasir. Your dad is steamin'. Whatever that guy Ken or Kenny did got him furious."

My phone alerted me that I had a text message as I was trying to soothe my mom's worries. It was from Leah. And the only reason I gave it my time was because I figured I could possibly use her to get to Kenny. Despite my mom's concerns, I had already made up my mind that Kenny needed to get what was comin' to him. That stunt he pulled in the hospital and then him admittin' to killin' Brock definitely put him on the hit list. And that wasn't even my thing, but certain niggas left you no other choice.

Nasir, in case I never see you again, I need you to know two things: 1) I never had an agreement with the cops to give info on you, your dad, or anybody you're affiliated with besides Kenny. I only told Kenny that so he wouldn't wonder how I got out of jail without posting bail. He's actually the one I've been informing against. When I left you at the hospital, I went straight to the police station and I told the cops about his involvement in Brock's and the cop's death, which explains why he was locked up at Brock's funeral. 2) I really love you and hope you can forgive me for the things that I did do wrong. And when it comes out that I'm tellin' the truth about this, I hope we can be friends again, if not for us, for the sake of our child. I'm pregnant, and in my heart I believe it's yours.

I rubbed my mom's shoulder and excused myself. I went into the half bath on the first floor. I was agitated by the text message because I didn't know if I could believe it or not. I didn't know if Leah was playin' me.

Kenny did get locked up at the funeral, and I hadn't said anything about him when the cops questioned me, so how else would they have known his involvement? But then again, who was to say that the cops locked him up on that? Kenny was in the streets heavy, so he could have gotten locked up on a number of charges.

But on another note, Leah did say that she couldn't leave Kenny because she was tied to him for reasons beyond her control. I was caught in the matrix. I didn't know what to believe, who to trust, what to do.

And the more I thought about things and tried to put all the pieces of the puzzle together, the more confused I became. On the one hand, I didn't think Leah was ever trying to set me up. I mean, she never pried for information. Plus, my pop and me wasn't doin' nothin' like that. On the other hand, I couldn't put shit past her.

Then this whole thing about her being pregnant threw me off. Why would she tell me that in a text? Why wouldn't she have told me when I saw her in person at the hospital? I had a lot of questions for Leah, too many to text. I called her. Fuck it. If Kenny was near her, she wouldn't have texted me.

The phone rang three times before somebody picked up. I waited to hear Leah's voice, and when I didn't I spoke, "Hello?"

I waited a few seconds for a response then I said hello again. No one responded still, but in the background I could hear screaming.

"KENNY, STOP, PLEEEEASE! KENNNNYYY!"

"Please, Kenny, don't kill me . . . Please."

My heart sank as I realized what I was hearing. I ran out the bathroom and toward the front door.

"Nasir, where you goin'?" my mom shouted out to me.

"To Leah's house! That nigga is goin' to kill her!"

My mom was yelling something to me, but I couldn't hear her. I jumped in my car and punched the gas. It was a challenge trying to drive with one good arm, especially while holding my phone to my ear. I managed to turn my blue tooth on so that I could free up my hand. As I was straining to hear what was bein' done to Leah, my other line started ringing. It was my mom. I ignored the call because I didn't want to disconnect with Leah. I didn't even want to hang up to call the police. And anyway, I didn't have Leah's address to give to the police if I did call. I just knew how to get to her house.

"This'll teach you to wear a wire on me, bitch!" I heard Kenny's voice in the distance.

Then I heard Leah's voice, and she was much clearer.

"The Lord is my shepherd; I shall not want. he maketh me to lie down in green pastures: he leadeth me beside the still waters. He restoreth my soul: he leadeth me in the paths of righteousness for his name's sake. Yea, though I walk through the valley of death, I will fear no evil: for thou art with me; thy rod and thy staff they comfort me. Thou preparest a table before me in the presence of mine enemies: thou anointest my head with oil; my cup runneth over. Surely goodness and mercy shall follow me all the days of my life, and I will dwell in the house of the Lord for ever."

I took a hard swallow. It became clear to me that what Leah had texted me was real and that it may indeed be the last time I got to hear from her. Tears actually formed in my eyes as I listened to her recite a Bible verse.

Having just laid my best friend to rest the day before and now hearing the one girl I can say I was in love with speak what sounded like her last words, my heart felt like it had literally broken. I'd never known such pain.

"LEAH!" I screamed with all my might. "LEAH, DON'T LEAVE ME LIKE THIS!"

CHASER

Leah

woke up to the sound of Nasir's voice. I lifted my arm and placed my cell phone as close to my ear as possible.

"Nasir?" I muffled, still somewhat dazed.

"LEAH!"

"Nasir? Am I in heaven?"

"No, baby. Heaven ain't ready for you yet. I need you to stay with me for a while. You hear me?"

"I must be in heaven if I'm talkin' to you."

Nasir said, "No, Leah. Look around you. You're home, right? Tell me you're at your house." His voice was cracking as if he was crying.

I opened my eyes, and although everything was blurry, I recognized where I was. "Yeah. I'm in the hall," I told him. My throat was so itchy.

"Okay, now who is there with you?"

"I don't see anybody. But"—I coughed—"it's smoky."

"Smoky? Like how smoky?"

I couldn't answer him because I couldn't stop coughing.

"LEAH! LEAH! GET YOURSELF TOGETHER, LEAH! CAN YOU MOVE? ARE YOU ABLE TO GET UP?"

I panicked as I grabbed the banister with my free hand and pulled myself over closer to the stairs. There was a fire in my living room.

My mind told me to run for a window, but my body wouldn't budge. I lost my self-control as I was filled with terror. I started screaming and crying at the same time.

"HELP ME! HELLLLPPP! SOMEBODY!!!!" I freaked out.

"LEAH! WHAT'S WRONG? WHAT DO YOU SEE?"

"NASIR, MY HOUSE IS ON FIRE! I CAN'T MOVE! I THINK MY LEGS ARE BROKEN! I CAN'T MOVE! I'M GOIN' DIE, NASIR!" I screamed and then began choking.

"NO! YOU'RE GONNA BE FINE! I'M FIVE MINUTES AWAY! NOW I NEED YOU TO CALM DOWN. I'M GONNA CALL THE POLICE ON MY THREE-WAY, OKAY? AND I'MA NEED YOU TO GIVE THEM YOUR ADDRESS!"

I heard Nasir, but I couldn't respond to him. My lungs were trying to fight the thick smoke that quickly clogged the air. I was choking to the point of vomiting.

"LEAH! STAY WITH ME!" I heard Nasir shout. I wanted to keep the phone to my ear, but I was feeling too weak. I was looking around for something to cover my nose with to keep from inhaling the smoke. I noticed my overnight bag on the top step. I tried sliding over to it. Meanwhile, I put Nasir on speakerphone and put my cell phone in my bra. That way I could use both my hands to get me across the floor.

"LEAH, ARE YOU STILL WITH ME?"

"I'm trying to get to air," I said, my voice growing more raspy.

CHASER

"Okay, okay. Good," Nasir said. I'm goin' to call—" *UUURRRRK-KKKK! BOOOOOOM!*

A loud crash interrupted Nasir's sentence. Before I could say anything, I heard another loud boom. That time, though, it didn't come from the other end of the phone. It came from downstairs.

"HELLLPPPP ME! HELLLPPPP ME!" I used all the energy I had left to scream.

I heard many deep voices giving commands back and forth. Then I heard footsteps rushing toward me. I cried at the sight of three firemen appearing through the smoke.

"Nasir!" I tried to yell. "Nasir! They're here!"

I didn't get a reply. In fact, I didn't hear anything coming from my phone. Nasir must have hung up.

I was carried out of my burning house and placed on a stretcher.

My eyes closing, I said, "I think my boyfriend was in a car accident. Can y'all send somebody to help him?"

At that, an oxygen mask was put over my nose and mouth. I was lifted into the back of an ambulance and given an IV. Moments later an overwhelming feeling of exhaustion came over me, and I closed my eyes.

Nasir

By the time my car had stopped spinning, police cars were already on the scene. That was a good thing, too, because I could get one of them to follow me to Leah's house before it was too late.

"Officer!" I shouted out as I limped toward the many cop cars that were blocking the intersection of Presidential Boulevard and City Avenue, some feet up from where my car was hit.

I had just gotten off the Lincoln Drive and was going through the light when a car came speeding off the expressway ramp, slamming into my passenger side. Apparently after the crash the driver of the other car coasted up the street some before the cops cut him off.

"Officer!"

"Freeze!" the cops yelled, pointing their guns.

I stopped and raised my one arm. *What the fuck,* I thought.

Then I noticed the driver of the other car slowly dropping to his knees, and I realized the cops weren't paying me any attention. Instead, they were all focused on the guy who was surrendering in the middle of the street.

The cops ran toward him, turned him around, and slammed him facedown on the ground so they could cuff him. I got a quick glance at the guy whose head was gushing out blood from the crash and wondered what the hell he had done that would make the cops more eager to arrest him than to get him to the hospital. Then I concluded that he must have been in a chase with them, which would have explained why he ran his light and hit me and why the cops were on the scene so fast.

I started walking toward the cops again.

"I need help! Officers!" I began to yell.

"Get back, sir," a white man met me as I was getting closer to the cops. He wasn't in a police uniform, but the gun and badge on his hip told me he was a cop.

"I need help! A girl's house is on fire! Her boyfriend tried to kill her! She lives around the corner! I need y'all to follow me over there before it's too late!" I rambled on.

The cop frowned and asked, "Are you talkin' about Leah Baker?"

"Yeah! She called me," I tried to explain as I patted my jeans pockets in search of my cell phone.

"Calm down, calm down," the cop said, his hand on my shoulder. "Ms. Baker has been taken to the hospital."

Instantly, I was able to relax some. But in seconds I was back to being worried.

"Well, is she okay? I mean, she sounded like she was dyin' on me."

The cop nodded and said, "She's doin' okay. Um, what is your name, sir?"

"Nasir," I said. "Nasir Freeman."

"And who are you to Ms. Baker?"

"A close friend. I was on my way to her house to help her when this idiot came out of nowhere and hit my fuckin' car!"

"Well, I'm glad the idiot hit you. Don't get me wrong. I'm glad you're not hurt. But that idiot is the boyfriend who tried to kill Ms. Baker. There's no tellin' how long we would have been chasin' him had it not been for you."

I was registerin' what the cop told me. When I realized that the guy the cops had apprehended was Kenny, I had mixed feelings. I was happy they caught him, but I wished I could have gotten to him first. And fuck fightin'. I would have tried to kill that nigga.

I dropped my head in my palm and stood there in the middle of the street gathering my thoughts. Once I was able to digest everything, I started thanking God repeatedly in my head. My heartbeat had begun to slow back down to normal. And it felt like a ton had been lifted off me. The crazy journey I had traveled with Leah and Kenny had come to an end. And I had to smirk that it had ended the same way it began—with an accident.

I asked if I could be taken to the hospital to see Leah. The cop said of course and reminded me that I needed to be seen and treated for injuries myself. Aside from minor scrapes and bruises, my shoulder was in a lot of pain.

An ambulance drove me to the University of Pennsylvania emergency room. I was given a bed next door to Leah. She wasn't in her room because she had to be taken to get chest X-rays and blood tests. But I felt good just to be next to her.

As soon as I got settled, I called my mom and dad to tell them what had happened. They were already en route to the hospital. Apparently they'd heard about the collision over the scanner, and then one of my dad's chasers called him and told him that it was my car that was in the accident.

I braced myself for what they were goin' to say and how they were goin' to feel about my decision to leave to help Leah without first running it by them. I could hear my mom: *You could've gotten seriously hurt or killed even.* And my dad: *How you know she wasn't tryin' to set you up? You know she can't be trusted.*

I knew I had it comin', but it didn't even matter. I knew the truth now, and I was content with it. I wanted to be with Leah despite my mom and dad's feelings about it, and with Kenny out of the picture, it would be more feasible. My mind was made up. It was what it was.

Leah

It was my last day in the hospital after having been in there for a week, longer than expected because I had developed pneumonia as a result of the smoke inhalation. My list of injuries included a miscarriage and two broken ribs due to the blows Kenny delivered to my stomach and chest. Surprisingly, I didn't feel sad or depressed, or even mad, for that matter. I guess I was just grateful to be alive.

I was sitting in the bed watching TV waiting for my doctor to come in with my discharge papers. The program I was watching had been interrupted by breaking news. Hillary Clinton had suspended her campaign and endorsed Barack Obama for the presidency. I shook my head. I couldn't believe a black man was running for president of the United States. I felt good about that and better about the fact that he actually had a chance of winning the election.

"Leah," I heard Detective Daily say just above a whisper.

I turned toward the door and smiled.

"Hello," I greeted him.

He still had sorrow in his eyes even after I had told him over and over again that I accepted his apology for not protecting me. It wasn't his fault. When I called him and asked if he had heard Kenny's confession, we both thought Kenny had gotten in the car with his brother and left. Neither of us knew that Kenny sent his brother ahead without him. So when the rental car pulled out of our garage, the cops followed it without hesitation. Neither they nor I had felt the need to have someone stay behind with me because Kenny was gone, so we'd thought.

But anyway, it was in the past. Lessons were learned, and fortunately lives were spared.

"I have some good news and bad news," the detective told me. "Which do you want first?"

I thought about it briefly and said, "Save the best for last."

"Well, the bad news is we most likely won't be able to get a conviction on Kenny for murdering my partner, Detective Marshall—"

"What? Why not?"

"His lawyer brought up some tactical issues about how we went about getting Mr. Courtland on a wire tap. There were some loopholes on our end, and he's going to request that that evidence be suppressed."

"That's crazy!" I was appalled. "So he'll just walk free, then?"

"Well, no. Here's the good news. With your testimony we will be able to convict him of first-degree murder of your unborn child."

My face wrinkled with confusion. "That's possible? Even though I didn't have the baby yet?"

Detective Daily nodded. "Pennsylvania passed a fetal-homicide bill acknowledging the unborn to be a human life from the moment of conception. So all we would need is your testimony and, of course, medical records and other physical evidence."

"Well, you'll have my testimony, Detective. That's a given."

The detective gently patted me on the shoulder and nodded. "Let's finally put this monster behind bars where he belongs," he said.

I nodded and, with tears in my eyes, responded, "Let's do it."

I needed a moment to myself after Detective Daily had given me the news about the possible ways of convicting Kenny. I couldn't believe that I had risked my life and lost my baby by wearing a wire and that the evidence we had gotten from it wouldn't even be permissible in court. However, it was gratifying knowing that Kenny would, indeed, be punished for taking my unborn baby's life. And that realization sent chills through me. It definitely made me look at abortions differently. And if I had it to do all over, I would have decided to keep my baby right off the bat.

By the time I was discharged, I felt like a whole different person. I felt more humbled. Small things that had mattered to me before no longer mattered. To me, breathing was a privilege. Life was a miracle. And every day was truly a gift.

My mom, who had visited me every day, practically become my caretaker and was there to accompany me to the hotel that the cops had arranged for me to stay in for the next month or so until it was time for me to testify at Kenny's trial.

While in the hotel, I got used to seeing the same faces I had seen every day while I was in the hospital: my mom, Detective Daily, the three cops who took turns watching over me twenty-four/seven, and the person I was most happy to see, Nasir.

For the next thirty days I concentrated on recovering and rested every chance I got. I didn't do too much thinking about testifying until the time for me to do so drew near. I got extremely nervous the day of the preliminary hearing. Up to the point that I was still second-guessing whether or not I wanted to testify. I hadn't seen Kenny since he had beaten me and set our house on fire, and I wasn't sure I was ready to face him in court.

Before we were scheduled to leave the hotel, there was a knock on the bathroom door.

"Come in," I said.

Through the mirror I saw Nasir. He wrapped his arm around me from behind and buried his head in the back of my neck.

"What's wrong?" I asked him.

"I wish I could trade places with you," he said. "I wish I could relieve you of this burden. I know you're scared to do this, and I feel like I want to be able to protect you from having to, but I can't. Just like I couldn't protect you from being hurt by that nigga. Just like I couldn't protect Brock and just like I couldn't protect our child . . ."

I turned to face him. Shaking my head, I explained, "You had no control over any of that. It was nothin' you could have done."

"That's the problem. I feel like it was. I shoulda been washed my hands of that nigga. And even now up to this day, I feel like I ain't doin' what I'm supposed to be doin'."

"And what is that, Nasir?" I asked him.

"I should be puttin' two in that nigga's head," Nasir said, gritting his teeth. "I feel like a real pussy right now, Leah. Like I'm takin' the easy way out by lettin' you take the stand."

"What do you mean the easy way out? This is by no means easy. Not for me or for you. So don't even say that. I think about what I shoulda done and what I coulda done, too, but at the end of the day what I did freed us both from Kenny, and I'll be damned if I let you jeopardize that."

"I understand all that, but it don't sit well with me. It hasn't since he got locked up. I mean, yeah, he's locked up, but it don't feel like he's gettin' his due for all the bullshit he put us through, Leah. It don't feel like revenge to me."

I grabbed Nasir's hand and squeezed it. "That's because you're not lettin' go and livin' your life. Let livin' be your revenge. 'Cause it's damn sure goin' be mine."

And with that I made Nasir's weakness my strength. I went to court with my head held high. I took the stand and gave my testimony with ease. I was able to look Kenny in his eyes and everything. I wanted him to see that he hadn't killed me at all, not physically and not emotionally, either. I had survived him.

When it was all said and done, I never had to step foot back in a courtroom again. Kenny's case never went to trial. After the preliminary hearing, I was told that Kenny took a plea deal. Instead of the twenty-five to life he would have gotten had he been found guilty, he was sentenced to twelve years. He thought he had got off good, too, until immediately after sentencing he was brought up on charges for the murder of Brakir "Brock" Jackson.

Nasir found a way to fulfill his urges of getting revenge. He came forward to police that Kenny admitted to him that he killed Brock. And being an eyewitness at the scene, Nasir agreed to testify against Kenny.

Kenny didn't take a plea. He wanted to fight the case, and he even tried to discredit Nasir by bringing up the fact that Nasir had been involved in a hit-and-run some years earlier. But the prosecution argued that Kenny's withholding that information about Nasir's hit-and-run made him an accessory to the crime. His dumb ass immediately withdrew his statement.

After a long, drawn-out trial, Kenny was found guilty on several counts, the biggest one being murder in the first degree.

He was sentenced to twenty-five to life, and it was to run consecutive with his prior sentence, which meant he was basically going to die behind bars.

Meanwhile, I ended up getting in touch with Sammy, Kenny's accountant, and getting all the money Kenny had left behind. It wasn't just handed over to me, of course. I had to threaten Sammy that I would go to the police with evidence that he had laundered money for Kenny. Sammy didn't want his ties to a cop killer made public, and he definitely wanted no part of jail, so he wound up complying with me.

I took the money and moved out of Philadelphia. I went somewhere where the weather was warm all year round—Orlando, Florida. With me, I took my mom and a promise from Nasir to join me as soon as Kenny's trial was over.

Leah

Some months later . . .

Where the hell is Nasir?" I looked at my watch. It was two
o'clock, an hour and a half after he was supposed to have arrived.

"Is that him?" my mom asked, looking past the crowd in front of
us at a guy walking quickly toward us.

I stood on my tippy toes to get a better look, and when I realized
it was, in fact, him, I met him in the crowd. I jumped in his arms and
held him tight for a minute before pulling away from him and asking,
"What happened to you? I thought you were goin' to stand me up. We
were about to go ahead with the opening ceremony without you!"

"Naw, they lost my luggage and I got held up at the airport," Nasir
explained.

"See," I said, leading him through the crowd to the position where

I had been standing before he got there. "That's why you should have flown in days ago."

"I wanted to, believe me. Shit, I'm lucky I made it down today. My mom and dad gave me hell about coming out here. I told them the story frontward and backward, over and over again, and they *still* have doubts about you. They think I'm movin' too fast by comin' down here. They still need time," Nasir told me.

"Well, what about you, Nasir? How do you feel? Do you still need time?"

Nasir looked around and said, "You got Disney World behind you, a bunch of excited kids in front of you, news cameras all around you, and a pair of big-ass scissors about to cut the ribbon, so I feel like you're official. Everything you've told me panned out. So no, I guess I don't need time." Nasir smiled.

On that note, I placed Nasir's hand on top of mine as I cut the big red ribbon at the grand opening of Fantasy Cut, my kids' salon and day spa, which sat on City Walk in the heart of Disney World. Cameras flickered and the crowd cheered as I opened the doors to the salon.

Inside, stylists dressed as characters such as Snow White and Cinderella were waiting to style the kids' hair. At each station was a Disney-themed TV/DVD combo, each playing a different Disney movie. Instead of regular barber and stylist chairs, the children sat in Disney-themed cars, trucks, and planes. There was even a horse and carriage for kids to sit in while they got styled at Cinderella's station. My mom, dressed as Sleeping Beauty, worked the reception desk. Nasir stood awestruck, watching me live out the dream I had first told him about over a year ago during one of our secret lunch dates back in Philly.

After the events of the day wound down, my mom went home while Nasir and I went out for drinks. Nasir bought a bottle of champagne and proposed a toast. We held our glasses up and looked into each other's eyes.

"Cheers to chasing freedom," I said.

"Cheers to chasing love," Nasir followed.

We clinked our glasses and sipped down our champagne. And at that very moment, I thought about everything I had been through and all that I had done to get to where I was. And I realized it had all been worth it. Indeed, the ends justified the means. The chase was worth the catch.

ACKNOWLEDGMENTS

To Allah for choosing this path for me. To everyone who has helped in the process of getting my sixth novel to the masses. To my family and friends for still putting the word out as if this were book one. And to my fans for allowing me to live my dreams.

Thank you!
Ya Girl